Restoreth My Soul

Other Books by Debbie Viguié

The Psalm 23 Mysteries

The Lord is My Shepherd
I Shall Not Want
Lie Down in Green Pastures
Beside Still Waters

The Kiss Trilogy

Kiss of Night
Kiss of Death

Sweet Seasons

The Summer of Cotton Candy
The Fall of Candy Corn
The Winter of Candy Canes
The Spring of Candy Apples

Witch Hunt

The Thirteenth Sacrifice
The Last Grave

Restoreth My Soul

Psalm 23 Mysteries

By Debbie Viguié

Published by Big Pink Bow

Restoreth My Soul

ISBN-13: 978-0615779492

Published by Big Pink Bow

www.bigpinkbow.com

This book is dedicated to Calliope Collacott for all her enthusiasm, passion, and support.

Although the job of writing a book can be incredibly lonely and isolating at times, there are those who touch our lives and ease our burden. I owe a tremendous debt of gratitude to the friends, family, and colleagues who have encouraged me and helped me on this journey. Thank you for all of your efforts to keep me sane and keep me writing! Love to you all.

1

Detective Mark Walters hated Tuesdays less than other days. Tuesdays were generally good days because it was the day the fewest people were murdered or committed suicide in total. That meant there were fewer new crime scenes to go to on Tuesdays so he could work on all of his other outstanding cases. Which was a good thing because the files were stacking up on his desk.

To make matters worse, some of the cases were considerably colder than when he'd last dealt with them. That was just one price for being away so long.

He was only three weeks back at work after having been on suspension for a few months. It still felt strange and it was going to take a while for the other officers to stop treating him like he had some kind of catching disease. On the whole, though, he was relieved to be back on the job, even though he kept finding himself staring at the empty desk of his dead partner, Paul.

There were half a dozen open cases in his inbox, all of them months old. There was a dead Iranian student, a murdered art dealer, and a man dead in a building fire that he may or may not have set himself among others. The only mystery that really had his attention, though, was the one involving Paul.

He had found out shortly after his partner was killed that Paul Dyer was an imposter who had taken the identity of the real Paul Dyer when they were both young children. The remains of the real Paul Dyer had been discovered in a mass grave at a popular camp in the woods and the true identity of his long-time partner was still a mystery.

The Dyer family refused to accept that the boy who had returned to them after their son had been kidnapped was not, indeed, their child. Only his sister was willing to believe the truth and she had already given him what little help she could.

Officially, the case of Paul Dyer was closed. Officers assigned to it after Mark's suspension had been unable to determine the identity of the man they had worked side by side with for years. But since they knew how he died and who killed him they had stopped looking.

Mark had spent the majority of his suspension scouring the internet for old reports of missing children trying to uncover the truth, but he had gotten nowhere. Either the records had never made it online for some reason, or no one had reported the boy missing in the first place.

"Walters!"

He looked up from the file he was poring over.

"Body over on Maple. Check it out."

He grabbed his jacket, took the piece of paper the other officer was holding, and headed out the door. Truth was, he was relieved to have something new to be working on. Hopefully it would take his mind off of everything else.

It didn't take him long to get to the house in question. It was a nice house, decent size, on a quiet street. The only thing that seemed amiss was the squad car parked in the driveway and the officer exiting the house and waving to him.

Mark parked on the street and got out, taking in more of the street. A neighborhood like this would likely be mostly upper middle class families. He pulled out his notebook and pen, ready to take notes.

The officer met him halfway to the door. Mark flashed his badge somewhat self-consciously.

"I know who you are, Detective," the officer, whose name tag said Liam, told him.

"And you're talking to me? I'm impressed," Mark said, unable to stop the sarcasm from rolling off his tongue.

"I might not like what you did, but I've no call to judge you. I wasn't there."

"Haven't walked a mile in my shoes and all of that?" Mark asked, looking more closely at the officer.

Liam looked like he was in his late twenties with red hair and blue-green eyes. He had the build of a football player, and he held himself with pride.

"Something like that, sir," Liam answered.

"I'll take what I can get. Tell me what happened."

"Anonymous call about some sort of disturbance here. Dispatch sent me."

"Where's your partner?"

"Just dropped him home with the stomach flu."

Mark wrinkled his nose, but didn't comment. "So, you got here."

"Yes, sir. I arrived and knocked on the front door, but no one answered."

"So, what sent you inside?" Mark asked.

"I heard a scream. I tried the door, found it unlocked, entered and announced myself."

Mark nodded. Liam had followed protocol. It was a good thing, but it just reminded Mark of his own failings. For a fleeting moment he wondered if he was truly fit to return to active duty and then instantly wanted to slap himself for the self-doubt.

"Did you find anyone?"

"Only the body, sir. I believe the scream was from one of two cats that was inside. They raced out when I opened the door and I haven't seen them since."

"So, no one in the house, just a body?"

"That's right, sir."

Mark couldn't take it anymore. "It's Detective or Mark. My father was 'sir'. Understand?"

"Yes, s-Detective."

"Alright, lead the way."

The first thing that struck Mark upon entering the house was how Spartan everything was. The dining room held a small table with two chairs. There were no pictures of any kind on the walls nor were there any in the hallways. The carpets looked practically new. As they moved farther into the house they passed a kitchen. It, too, looked like it hadn't really been lived in. There were no small appliances on the counter, not even a coffee maker. These were all swept clean as though this was a freshly built house.

"The owner isn't much for decorating," Mark noted.

Liam coughed. "Not in the traditional sense."

Mark was about to ask him what he meant when Liam led him into what was probably the living room.

Mark stopped and stared, amazed. There was a body crumpled in the corner, and a bright red smear of

4

symbols on the wall immediately above it. He thought for just a moment that the walls were painted black with speckling but then realized that they were covered in more symbols, these tiny and in black.

He stepped farther in the room and then turned and took it all in. Every square inch of every wall was covered in the same. He approached the body and looked down. A little old man, in his upper eighties at least, his bright blue eyes were fixed in death.

"He has to be in his eighties, at least," Mark noted.

He glanced at the bright red symbols on the wall just above the body. They looked like somebody had written in red paint and let it run down. He leaned closer and sniffed at it.

"This looks like blood," he noted.

"That was my thought as well," Liam said, crouching down beside him. "And look, there's blood on the fingers of his right hand."

"So there is," Mark said. "Forensics can sort all this out for sure, but for the moment let's assume that he wrote this in blood. What was so important to him?"

"I don't know," Liam said earnestly.

Mark hid a smile. The question had been rhetorical but it was clear that the officer wanted to help.

"What's the rest of the house look like?" Mark asked, not yet ready to go see for himself, but wanting the information.

"There's a bedroom off to the side down here. It's got a bed and a dresser. Shaving gear and toothbrush in the bathroom."

"And upstairs?"

"Three rooms, all of them empty."

"Completely empty?"

Liam nodded. "I opened the closets in my sweep to make sure no one was hiding in them."

"Good work," Mark said.

He stared intently at the bloody symbols. They were written over the top of more of the tiny black symbols. They looked like they might almost be some kind of writing and he felt that perhaps he had seen it somewhere before.

He turned and looked at Liam who was watching him intently, clearly waiting for instructions.

Mark stood up. "Secure the perimeter."

Liam jumped up. "I'm on it."

"Oh, and one other thing."

"Yes, Detective?"

Mark pointed to the symbols. "What is that?"

"It looks like Hebrew," Liam offered.

Hebrew, that made sense. Mark squinted at it.

"Can you read it?"

The officer shook his head.

"Can you think of anyone in the department who is Jewish or might have studied Hebrew for any reason?"

Again Liam shook his head.

"Neither can I," Mark said with a frustrated sigh.

He stepped up even closer to the one wall and stared at it intently for a moment while Liam went outside to work on securing the perimeter.

Whatever it was, it was clearly important to somebody. The sooner he could get it translated the sooner he might be able to figure out exactly what had been going on here.

There was one person he knew who could help him out with that.

"I can't believe I'm doing this," Mark muttered to himself as he pulled out his phone.

A few seconds later Rabbi Jeremiah Silverman answered.

"Hi, Rabbi," Mark said, feeling awkward and deciding to use Jeremiah's title.

"What can I do for you, Detective?"

"I just found a dead body."

There was a pause and then Jeremiah asked, "Why are you calling me?"

"Well, it's been a few months since either you or the secretary found a dead body so I figured it was past time we all gathered around a corpse," he said sarcastically, hating himself for having called in the first place.

"And the real reason would be?"

Mark sighed. "I could use some help. There's writing all over the wall in the room in which we found the victim. Only trouble is, it looks like it's written in Hebrew."

"And you don't know anyone who can translate it?"

"Sure I do. I'm calling him right now."

Mark swore he heard an audible sigh. Anyone else and he wouldn't have asked, but he and the rabbi had too much history at this point for him to waste a perfectly good resource by not trying to get him to help. Besides, all he needed him to do was translate, it wasn't like he was involving him in yet another one of the crimes that he and the secretary seemed to be stumbling into all the time.

Paul would have hated it. He hated dealing with Jeremiah and Cindy and would always reference them as 'civilians'. Paul wasn't there to complain, though, no matter how much Mark wished he was.

"What's the address?" Jeremiah asked after a minute.

Mark couldn't help himself. "I knew you couldn't resist the chance to get involved, Samaritan."

The name was an old joke between them.

"How many times must I remind you, I'm Jewish."

Mark smiled. The whole world had been turned upside down for him, but it was good to know that some things never changed.

Jeremiah hung up from talking with Mark. He had been doing hospital visitations early in the morning and had just gotten into the synagogue. Now it seemed he was heading right back out.

He walked out of his office and into the main reception area just as his secretary, Marie, appeared from the direction of the copy machine.

"Rabbi, I didn't hear you come in," she said.

"Unfortunately, I have to go right back out," he said.

She frowned. "When will you be back?"

"I'm not sure. This could take a little while and then I have a lunch appointment."

"I didn't see anything on your calendar." Her eyes narrowed suddenly. "It's not with that Gentile woman is it?"

"Marie, I promise that you're the only person in America who uses that word," Jeremiah said with a sigh.

"I knew it. You should be careful," she said, wagging a finger at him. "Tongues may talk."

"Thanks for the warning, Marie. Anything else?"

"Yes, there was a package here this morning when I arrived. It had your name on it," she said, pointing to a very large, flat parcel wrapped in brown paper and leaning against one wall.

"Who is it from?"

"I don't know."

"What is it?"

"I don't know, but it felt like a picture of some sort when I moved it."

Jeremiah walked over and picked it up. It did feel like some sort of art or picture. He moved it into his office and then locked the door.

"I'll be in late this afternoon if anyone needs me," he said as he walked out the door.

She sniffed loudly, but didn't say anything else. He was grateful for the small miracle.

Outside by his car he glanced over at the neighboring parking lot for the church where Cindy worked. He had figured they'd meet in the parking lots that were separated by just a small hedge and drive to lunch in one car. He might have to meet her at the restaurant now, it depended on how long Mark kept him. He'd text her when he figured it out.

It took him fifteen minutes to drive to the address Mark had given him. Pine Springs was a nice community, about an hour away from Los Angeles. The best thing about it was that, unlike L.A., nothing was too far away.

He parked across the street from a small house that already had police tape surrounding it. He took a deep breath. He always hated getting involved with police investigations. They set him on edge.

He glanced at the clock and resigned himself to the fact that he'd have to meet Cindy at the restaurant instead of picking her up. He texted her before climbing out of the car and walking slowly up to the house.

A couple of police officers he recognized didn't even give him a second glance. He gritted his teeth. The fact that they were that comfortable with his presence wasn't a good thing. He'd become far too involved.

There was nothing he could do about that now, though. A few months before he had thought about moving, relocating perhaps to a different state. Things were getting more and more complicated for him here. Thanks to his friendship with Cindy, though, he had decided not to move, even though it was the wiser course of action.

Mark met him outside the house, extending his hand.

Jeremiah shook, taking silent note of the formality of the greeting.

"Thanks for coming," Mark said.

"I'll do what I can to help."

"Since you're officially going to be a consultant-"

Jeremiah raised his hands. "I don't want to be an official anything. I'm just here to help a friend."

"Okay, but if anyone asks, you're a consultant."

"How does it feel, being back on the job?" Jeremiah asked.

Mark actually flushed. "Good, real good," he said gruffly.

Thanks to an unfortunate incident back in March, Mark had been suspended from the police department. He'd only been reinstated a few weeks before after going through extensive counseling with Jeremiah who had then signed off on the paperwork declaring the detective fit to return to duty.

"They assign you a new partner yet?"

"Not yet. I'm odd man out at the moment until we get someone else into the department. So, how is the secretary?" he said, obviously trying to deflect by changing the subject.

"Cindy and I are having lunch today. I'll be sure to find out for you."

"So, things are getting serious between you two."

"We're just friends."

Mark snorted derisively. "I've seen the way you look at each other. That's not friendship. That's a ticking time bomb waiting to explode."

It was Jeremiah's turn to be made intensely uncomfortable by the direction of the conversation.

"So, you wanted me to translate something?"

Mark grunted and turned to lead the way inside.

Jeremiah followed him, steeling himself for whatever it was he was about to encounter. The detective had said that there was Hebrew writing on the walls.

That meant there was a good chance either the victim or the killer or both were Jewish. He reminded himself that he had a role to play inside. He couldn't be too callous, he had to show some sensitivity to whatever it was he saw. It would be dangerous to do otherwise.

Inside the house they bypassed a dining room on the left and continued heading farther into the house. Inside what was meant to be a living room was where all the activity seemed to be happening.

Jeremiah stepped into the room. It was devoid of furniture. The walls were covered with writing, all of it in Hebrew, and most of the letters only about an inch high.

He whistled softly. "You didn't say how much translation work you were going to need."

"Want to re-open that whole consultant discussion?" Mark asked.

"Maybe," Jeremiah muttered as he moved his eyes around the walls. Almost all of the writing seemed to be done in black marker but as his eyes reached the last wall and moved down it there was a sudden patch of large letters written in what he was pretty sure was blood.

Below it was the body of a man.

"Did he write that?" Jeremiah asked, pointing to the large letters.

"We think so. There's blood on his hands. The lab guys will check it out but I'm guessing he used his own blood."

Jeremiah stepped forward, wondering what was so important the man had used his dying moments to write the letters.

"Can you make any of it out?" Mark asked.

"Well, the blood letters translate as 'restoration'."

"Restoration? Are you sure?"

"Yes."

"What do you think he meant by that?"

Jeremiah was about to tell him that he had no idea when his eyes fell on the body and he froze. For once he didn't have to feign shock or surprise.

"You okay?" Mark asked.

Jeremiah's mind raced, wondering exactly what he should tell the detective standing next to him. A dozen scenarios played out in his mind and at last he finally opted for the truth.

He turned to Mark and looked him square in the eyes as he answered his question.

"No, I'm not okay. I know this man."

2

Cindy Preston pulled her cell out of her purse. Jeremiah had sent her a text saying he'd meet her at the restaurant. She felt a twinge of disappointment. She enjoyed it when they drove together. It gave them a few extra minutes to spend together talking. They talked about all sorts of things like work, religion, music, and her childhood. The one topic they never touched on was his past. She had begun to notice that anytime she asked a question that was even tangentially related to his life before becoming the rabbi at the synagogue next door that he would steer the question away.

One of these days she was going to press him harder. She knew several people who didn't like talking about themselves but with Jeremiah it was ridiculous. The only thing she knew about his earlier life was that he had been raised in Israel and therefore spent a couple of years in the military as all young Israelis were required to do.

"Is it a text from Jeremiah?" Geanie asked teasingly as she leaned over Cindy's desk. "What does lover boy have to say?"

"We're just friends," Cindy said with a sigh.

"Right," Geanie said with a roll of her eyes as she walked over to her desk.

Geanie was the church's resident tech guru and the most outlandish character in a staff full of characters. Today she was wearing black fishnet stockings, four inch fuchsia heels, a black leather miniskirt and a fuchsia satin blouse. It was actually one of her more conservative looks.

Geanie was smiling and humming to herself. She did that a lot ever since she had become engaged to Joseph, one of the church members and a friend of Cindy's. The engagement and subsequent wedding planning were taking up all of her free time and the house that she and Cindy shared was littered with bridal magazines. Geanie's preoccupation with the subject and her own state of soon to be wedded bliss had caused her to see romance everywhere, even when it clearly didn't exist.

Jeremiah and I are just friends, Cindy repeated silently to herself.

Four more months and Geanie would be getting married and moving out and Cindy would once again be living by herself. She had just started getting used to having a roommate, too.

The office door opened and in walked Dave Wyman, the youth pastor who was more commonly referred to as Wildman. His face bore a look of pure frustration that she hadn't seen since the week before the high school summer camp. In fact for the past month he had walked around looking serene, a rarity for him. Then again, most everyone had. August at the church was usually dead with families taking their last vacations before school got back in.

Now it was September, though. Kids were back in school and the pews would be filling back up. Still, most of the major church activities wouldn't start back up again for a few weeks.

"What's wrong?" Cindy asked.

Wildman stopped and stared at her like he didn't even know where to begin.

"Your big back to school outreach nights aren't for another two weeks, right?" she asked.

He nodded.

And then she realized why he had that singular look of rage and despair mixed together. He was used to reigning supreme over organized chaos, taking the drama and crisis of teenage life in his stride. There was only one thing she knew of that could push him that far over the edge.

"Royus?" she asked, praying she was wrong.

He nodded and she felt her spirits plummet.

Roy the head pastor and Gus the music director couldn't stand each other. Most days they tried to stay out of each other's way, but sometimes that just wasn't possible. Worse, some days their feud spilled over onto others and the rest of the staff called that kind of problem a Royus.

"What happened?" Geanie asked, voice tense. A Royus was enough to cause even Cindy's free-spirited, love obsessed roommate more than a little stress.

Wildman slumped down in the chair near Cindy's desk and buried his head in his hands. "They're fighting over the Christmas pageant," he said, voice muffled.

Cindy turned and shared a bewildered look with Geanie. "Why? Normally they don't even start discussing Christmas until October."

"I know, but this year Gus wants to shake things up, do something different. He wants all new sets, backdrops, the works."

Cindy felt like she was going to be sick. "You have to be kidding."

"No. And he dragged me into the meeting, without warning me, by the way, because he wants the teens to have a bigger part in the whole thing."

"He didn't!" Geanie burst out.

"Oh yes he did. Then Roy accused him of trying to destroy our traditions and he told me that I should know better and that there's no way I could control the kids."

Cindy put a hand to her mouth. Horror for Dave and for the rest of them was filling her.

"Then I told him this wasn't my idea and it was the first I heard about it, which just made Gus go off on how I should have more faith in my kids and I should try to make them more a part of the congregation instead of isolating them like a bunch of lepers."

Cindy got up and gave Dave a hug. "I'm so sorry," she said.

He shuddered. "It's hard enough to put up with all the crap that comes with this job without having both of them drag me into the middle of their problems and yell at me for half an hour."

"What did you do?" she asked as she pulled away.

He looked up at her and then at Geanie and the despair in his eyes broke her heart. "I told them that if they both didn't knock it off they wouldn't have to worry about what I would or wouldn't do, because I would quit."

In the silence that followed his pronouncement Cindy heard Geanie drop a pen on the floor. She didn't glance over, she couldn't take her eyes off the youth pastor's face.

She licked her lips, feeling that she had to say something to make this better. "Look, I know it's been a rough year-"

"Rough?" he asked with a harsh laugh. "That doesn't even begin to describe it. First there was the spring camp debacle with the assassins trying to take out my kids and one of my counselors."

Cindy's fists tightened. She remembered the events all too well. Everyone who had been even remotely involved had been scarred by it.

"Then was the whole huge debate over whether to even have summer camps, and then where to have them since the police still had our old campsite locked down and none of the kids or counselors wanted to go back there anyway."

"I know a lot has happened, but you can't quit," Cindy interrupted.

Dave heaved a sigh. "Why do they have to be that way? I mean, we work at a church, shouldn't we be better than that?"

Geanie was out of her chair now, too, and she came to stand beside Cindy. "Yes, we all work at a church," she said softly, "but we're all still human and flawed."

Cindy couldn't have said it better herself.

"It's just hard to deal with them, especially when they're like this," Dave said.

"I know, we've all been there," Cindy said, "but you can't let them drive you away. The kids love you and they need you."

"I know, it's just, some days I feel like this job should come with hazard pay."

"Amen," Cindy couldn't help but respond.

He looked up at her and the faintest smile touched his lips. "I guess no one knows that better than you."

She smiled back.

"Don't let them get you down," Geanie said. "It could always be worse. You could be Cindy who's going to have to go fifteen rounds with them over the scheduling for December."

Cindy glared at Geanie. "That wasn't nice."

"No, but it does make me feel a little better," Dave said as he stood up.

Cindy raised an eyebrow. "Then maybe this will make you feel a lot better. It could be worse. You could be Geanie and have to try to come up with advertisements that they both sign off on. If there is a new program this year, that will even mean a whole new design aesthetic for them to argue over."

"I kind of hate you right now," Geanie said as she hunched her shoulders.

Dave grinned.

"You're looking better now," Cindy noted.

"What can I say, ladies? I guess it's true that misery loves company." He left the office and Cindy and Geanie both returned to their desks.

"That I didn't need," Cindy said with a sigh.

"Who did?" Geanie asked looking glum.

"I'm sorry, that wasn't nice of me to say. But you shouldn't worry. Everyone always loves everything you do. You've got the magic touch when it comes to your advertising."

"That's not what's worrying me," Geanie said.

"What is it then?"

The other girl looked up at her with despair filled eyes. "Both Roy and Gus are doing something for my wedding."

Even though it was wrong, Cindy almost couldn't control the urge to laugh.

Mark stared at Jeremiah in surprise. "You know him? Who is he?"

Jeremiah looked bewildered and Mark registered it was the first time he'd seen him look that way.

"I honestly can't tell you. All I know is that he came up to me after services one day in May, said he wanted to come into my office a couple days later to talk to me, and he never showed up. Frankly, I've always wondered what happened to him. He never told me his name."

"Did he tell you what he wanted to talk about?"

"No."

"How long did you talk with him after services?"

"Literally less than a minute."

Mark raised an eyebrow. "He must have made an impression for you to remember him so clearly."

Jeremiah kept his eyes fixed intently on the dead man. "He did. He was speaking a mixture of English and German."

"German?" Mark asked.

The rabbi nodded.

To the best of Mark's knowledge there wasn't any real German community nearby. He looked again at the body of the old man then lifted his eyes to take in the Hebrew lettering all over the walls. A terrible thought came over him. He put a pair of gloves on and he bent down slowly. He gingerly pushed up the man's sleeves on both arms, looking for a mark.

"I'm not convinced he was Jewish and I don't think he was in a concentration camp during the war," Jeremiah said quietly.

"There are no numbers tattooed on him so you're probably right about that," Mark said. "How did you know that was what I was looking for?"

Jeremiah shrugged. "German language, Hebrew writing, his age, it was a logical conclusion."

Mark stood up. "Maybe you're in the wrong line of work. You should have been a detective."

Jeremiah smiled faintly. "No, that's definitely not for me. I'll leave the detective work to the professionals."

"Because you've done such a good job of doing that in the past," Mark said, not bothering to hide the sarcasm in his voice. He took a deep breath. "What makes you think he wasn't Jewish?"

"I saw him at services and he didn't wear a kippah, even during prayer."

"Kippah?" Mark asked. "What's that?"

"Oh, you would call it... a yarmulke."

"Oh, the skull cap," Mark said, making a circle on the top of his head.

"Yes. Of course, not all Jewish men wear them, but it is very unusual to see a man of his age not wearing one, particularly during prayer. Hence my conclusion that he wasn't actually Jewish."

"Why do you wear those things?" Mark asked. He'd always wondered, but it wasn't something that usually came up in conversation.

21

"It's out of reverence, an acknowledgement that there is something higher than man, that being G-d, of course."

"Of course," Mark said. "So, how long do you think it's going to take you to translate this?" he asked, changing the topic.

Jeremiah turned and surveyed the rest of the room. "All of this? I really don't know."

"Then I guess you'd better get started."

"You're serious? You want me to translate all of this?" the rabbi asked.

Mark shrugged. "Hopefully something in it will give us a clue. Until then, we've got nothing to go on."

Jeremiah sighed and pulled out his phone. "Looks like I'll be missing lunch."

"I'll get you lunch. Anything else you need?"

"A ladder and a tape recorder. It will be far easier to just read the translation into that than to have to write it down."

"Done. First can you tell me what a line or two of this says? I'm curious if he's just been ranting something repetitive or crazy. You know like 'All work and no play.'"

The rabbi touched his hand to a section of the wall well above the bloody red letters. He read out loud slowly, making sure to read verbatim and not clean up the grammar or anything. "Twenty years ago since I lost my wife yet I miss her still. G-d has a reason for everything that is done. Why do not ask of me."

He fell silent for a moment and then turned to the detective. "Maybe it's his autobiography," he suggested.

Mark sighed. "And he couldn't put it on paper like a normal person."

Jeremiah sighed. "I don't think there was anything normal about this man."

"From what I've seen so far, I'd have to agree with you. Give me a minute and I'll get you the things you need."

"This is going to take a couple of days."

"Whatever it takes. Hopefully it will help us find a killer."

"I'm glad at least one of us is optimistic," Jeremiah said, eyeing the walls and sounding dubious. "I'll have Marie clear my schedule. I have to warn you, though. I've only got three days I can spend on this. After that I'm booked solid with the holidays."

"Which holidays?"

"The High Holy Days is probably how you've heard of them. It starts with Rosh Hashanah and ends with Yom Kippur."

"Isn't that a day for atonement?"

"Yes," Jeremiah said, clearly startled.

"Don't look so surprised. My wife made me watch that Jazz Singer movie."

Mark headed outside while the rabbi made his calls and found Liam outside. Other officers were starting to arrive and the medical examiner pulled up and got out of the car. All of them were civil with their greetings, but they still avoided making eye contact with him.

He tried not to let it get to him as he brought everyone up to speed. Once the medical examiner had headed inside he turned to Liam.

"I need a ladder and a tape recorder to help with the translation."

"You've got it," the younger officer said. "I'll be back as fast as I can."

"Can you pick up some Togo's sandwiches, too?"

"Not a problem," Liam said with a smile.

At least there was one guy on the force who wasn't treating him like a pariah.

Jeremiah felt terrible as he ended his call with Cindy. She'd sounded like she wasn't having the best of mornings and she'd been clearly disappointed that he wasn't going to make lunch. He knew how she felt. There were so many things he'd rather be doing than translating the dead man's writings and spending time with her was at the top of that list.

More police showed up and began to examine the body and take pictures of the room. He tried to stay out of the way while reading snatches of information from the walls. It did indeed seem to be some kind of autobiography and it seemed like everything was in order which was a stroke of luck that he couldn't quite believe.

He identified the wall with the blood on it as the last wall and found what seemed to be the first wall. The room continued to get more crowded and he finally walked outside where he found Mark sitting on the curb jotting down some notes.

"I was in the way," Jeremiah explained as he took a seat beside him.

Mark nodded. "I know the feeling."

"Want to talk about it?"

"No."

"Good."

That made Mark smile. "Don't worry. They'll clear out of there soon enough and the place will be all yours."

"Can't wait to be all alone in a dead man's house reading his life story," Jeremiah said, letting the sarcasm through.

A squad car pulled up and an officer Jeremiah had seen earlier got out. He made a beeline for Mark and handed him a digital recorder which he in turn handed to Jeremiah. Jeremiah tucked it into his shirt pocket where it fit comfortably.

"I've got the ladder in the trunk," the officer said.

"Thanks, Liam," Mark responded.

Liam held out a brown paper bag which Mark took from him. "Togo's sandwiches, the best you can get. I had him get roast beef."

He handed a sandwich to Jeremiah who thanked him.

"I know it's not lunch with your lady love, but at least it's something."

Jeremiah knew from experience that any protestations or sarcasm would just egg Mark on so he let it go without comment. He tore into the sandwich and had to admit that Mark was right about how good it was. The meat was flavorful and the bread was incredibly fresh but still substantial, like bread should be. He ate slowly, focusing on each bite. He had a lot of work ahead of him that he wasn't looking forward to so he tried to stay in the moment, focusing on the good.

Finally he was done and there was no delaying anymore. The body had been removed a few minutes before and almost everyone was clearing out. He stood reluctantly. "Time to get to work."

Liam got the ladder for him and carried it inside, setting it up where Jeremiah instructed. Mark trailed inside. "Are you going to be okay?" he asked.

"I don't need a babysitter, if that's what you're asking."

Mark nodded. "If you read anything interesting, call me."

"Will do, Detective," Jeremiah said.

He climbed up on the ladder and got as comfortable as he could as he found the first sentence in the room. He turned on the recorder and began to translate into it.

"My name is Heinrich Beck. I was born in Hamburg, Germany. My parents owned a small brewery."

Jeremiah hit pause and looked down at Mark. "At least you have a name if you didn't before. That is assuming the dead guy is the same one who wrote this. Given the bloody letters I'm guessing he is."

"And you're right, he's from Germany," Mark said with a grunt.

"You want to stay and hear the rest?"

"No, I've got to follow up on a few other things. Like I said, though, call if you get anything of interest."

"I will," Jeremiah said.

"Call when you're leaving tonight and I'll come by."

Jeremiah nodded and turned back to the wall.

A few minutes later Mark and the other officers cleared out leaving Jeremiah alone with the words of a dead man. He worked as fast as he could, but he had to keep moving the ladder. It was getting tiresome and the strain was beginning to take a toll.

He finally took a break and walked around the rest of the downstairs. It was amazing to him how barren, sterile, the rest of the house seemed. In the dining room his eyes gravitated to a tiny speck of black on a far wall. He walked over and inspected it. It turned out to be a small hole, probably left by a nail.

Something was hanging here once, he realized.

He wondered what it could have been. A painting, maybe a family portrait. It could have been a picture of Heinrich's wife.

Jeremiah touched the wall, wondering where whatever it had been was now. He was about to turn and head back to work when he thought he heard something. He stopped, straining his ears to listen.

It came again, a step, very faint, outside.

Was one of the officers coming back to gather more evidence?

He could hear more steps now, quiet, as though someone were trying to be furtive.

Maybe the police weren't the only ones interested in how Heinrich had died or what mysteries the walls of writing held.

Whoever it was they were just on the other side of the front door now. Jeremiah flattened himself against the wall, waiting for them to try the doorknob.

Moments later the knob turned slowly and Jeremiah coiled all his muscles, preparing to strike if need be. The door was shoved open and he saw a figure standing there, holding something large in front of them. He lunged forward as a woman screamed.

3

A figure lunged at her and Cindy screamed. The pizza box she had in her hands went crashing to the floor as something hit it. She threw her hands up in front of her face to ward off the impending attack.

It didn't come.

"Cindy?"

She lowered her hands slowly. "Jeremiah?"

He was standing, looking at her in surprise, and she realized he had been the one who had lunged out at her. "What are you doing?" she gasped.

"You startled me. I thought maybe you were the killer coming back to search the house or something," he admitted.

"I was bringing you a pizza for dinner since we missed out on lunch," she said. It sounded ludicrous, but it was true.

"How did you know where to find me?" he asked.

"Mark called and let me know."

"What, why?"

"I don't know."

She dropped her eyes to the pizza, feeling slightly dazed. There were cold sodas in a bag still hanging from her elbow along with her purse and they jostled her ribs.

They just stood and stared at each other for a moment. Cindy's heart was still pounding in her chest and Jeremiah looked incredibly tense. Then, slowly, a smile spread across his face.

"I'm glad you came," he said as he bent down and retrieved the pizza box.

"Good," she said, smiling in return.

"Sorry about that. Being here alone made me jumpy I guess."

"Oh, with good reason. Everything we've experienced. I should have knocked or something, but I felt weird enough ducking under the police tape and I wasn't sure what the procedure was."

"It's my fault. Now that you're here, though, let's get busy on this pizza. I'm starving."

Jeremiah led the way further into the house. The first thing she noticed was the lack of pretty much anything.

"Is this house up for sale or something?"

"Apparently not. He just lived like this."

"Bizarre."

He turned and looked at her. "No, you haven't seen bizarre yet."

She followed him into a room with what seemed to be black walls and she stopped in her tracks as she realized the walls were actually covered in writing. "You're right, this is definitely more bizarre."

She took a closer look at the tiny letters. "Mark wants you to translate all of this?" she asked in amazement.

"Yeah, lucky me," he said.

"But that's going to take forever."

"It's certainly feeling like it," he said.

She turned and saw the taped outline of a body on the carpet. She felt her stomach twist. On the wall there were letters spelled out in red that had to be blood.

"I'm sorry, let's go back to the kitchen," Jeremiah said quickly, peering at her with concerned eyes.

She managed a wan smile. "Yeah, soda goes better with pizza than blood does."

They backtracked to the kitchen and Jeremiah set the pizza box down on the counter. Cindy took the Cokes out of the bag while he lifted the lid. "Smells delicious."

She smiled, still slightly jittery. "How are things going here?"

"Tiring and so far fairly boring. I have a feeling I'm just about to get to the interesting parts, though. He's starting to talk about World War II."

"So, what exactly happened here?"

"We're not getting involved," he said as he grabbed a piece of pizza.

"You mean aside from you translating that entire room, at police request," she said, keeping her voice neutral.

For a moment she wasn't sure if he was going to smile or scowl, but finally the corners of his mouth jerked upward.

"Okay, fine. All we know about the dead guy so far is his name and that he was born and raised in Germany. He appears to have written the word restoration in his own blood as he was dying."

"Restoration? He was dying and that's the word that he bothered to write? Not the name of his killer or a goodbye to someone?" she asked. "That seems weird."

"I thought so, too," Jeremiah said, his forehead creasing in thought. "You know what else is weird?"

"What?" Cindy asked, grabbing her own slice of pizza. She took a bite and savored it.

"I actually met him once before."

"Where?" she blurted out with her mouth still full. She covered her hand with her mouth, embarrassed at herself.

Jeremiah didn't seem to care about her lack of manners. Then again, the two of them had been through so much maybe they were well beyond that point. The thought gave her a warm feeling inside.

"Memorial Day weekend at the Synagogue," he said.

The warm feeling was quickly doused by what felt like ice water rushing through her veins. She still felt a little sick to her stomach when she thought about what had happened to her on vacation in Hawaii and she still had nightmares where she saw Jeremiah starting to drown.

She shook her head, trying to clear it of the images that tormented her more often than she would ever admit. Again Jeremiah didn't seem to notice her distress, clearly lost in his own memories.

"He came up to me after services, shook my hand and told me how important he thought it was that we had met. He wanted to talk to me, but he seemed to be worried about people overhearing the conversation. We scheduled an appointment for that Wednesday, but he wouldn't give me his phone number or any way to reach him."

"And you missed that appointment because you were busy rescuing me," she said, guilt surging through her.

"Apparently he missed it, too. Marie said he never showed up and I hadn't seen or heard from him since. He seemed so insistent, though, that it was important. And he spoke German when he was flustered."

He turned and looked at her. "Are you okay?"

She set her slice of pizza down and nodded around the lump in her throat. "I'm glad that he didn't make the meeting either. I would hate to think that he needed your help and because of me-" she broke off, unable to continue.

Jeremiah dropped his slice onto the pizza box and put his hands on her face, tilting her eyes up to meet his. "Listen to me. What happened to him had nothing to do with you. Or with me. He broke the appointment, too, and he's had months to reach back out, but he hasn't. This is just some terrible coincidence here. You already carry around more guilt than you deserve, don't you even think about adding this to it."

"Thank you," she whispered.

He continued to stare at her and she felt like he was looking into her very soul. Jeremiah seemed to understand her on a much deeper level than anyone ever had.

"And even if this isn't a coincidence, it doesn't matter. You are the most important person in my life," he said.

Her breath caught in her throat and she became intensely aware of his hands pressing against her cheeks, the warmth radiating from his body as he stood so close to her. She stared deeply into his eyes and felt tears begin to sting her own as the truth took her by storm. "You're the most important person in my life, too," she whispered.

"Good, then we have an understanding," he said, expression intense.

Then he dropped his hands and took a small step backward. She felt her heart beginning to pound all over again. Just what kind of understanding did he think they had?

He resumed eating and after a moment so did she.

They finished dinner in silence, each lost in their own thoughts. After Jeremiah had drank the last of his soda he gave her a lopsided grin. "No rest for the wicked, isn't that what they say? I think it's time for me to get back to work."

Cindy followed him back into the other room. The sun was sinking in the sky and the room was getting darker. The seemingly endless summer days were beginning to grow shorter and soon winter would be upon them. Jeremiah flicked on the overhead lights in the room and she was glad to see that they provided more than enough light for him to continue to work by.

He pushed a ladder to the side. "I've finally reached the place where I can read the letters while standing on the ground," he explained.

"That's got to be a relief," she said.

"More than you can guess."

He pulled out his recorder and began to translate. She listened as she took a closer look around the room. He hadn't asked her to leave and she was in no mood to, not after whatever it was had just happened in the kitchen. Every time she started to think about it, though, she felt like she was having trouble catching her breath. Maybe it was best not to think too closely on it or read too much into it.

She saw the bloody word that he had said meant restoration. She still couldn't fathom why someone who was dying would choose to make that his last word.

"Jeremiah?"

He paused and she glanced at him. He pushed a button on the digital recorder. "What is it?"

"You said he was born and raised in Germany and that he spoke German when he was agitated?"

"Yes."

"And all of this is Hebrew. Was he Jewish?"

"Mark asked the same question and I told him I was almost certain that he wasn't."

"Then why bother learning Hebrew? I mean, it's not the easiest language in the world. You have to learn a completely different alphabet and teach yourself to write backward, from right to left, don't you?"

"That's correct."

"Why bother if you weren't Jewish?"

"Maybe he was some sort of scholar," he suggested.

"I guess that could be true," she said. It didn't feel right, though.

"If he is, I'm sure we'll find out when we get to that part of his story," Jeremiah said.

She continued to stare at the bloody letters on the wall. She knew what it was like to believe that your life was ending, that you were dying. She knew the pain, the fear, the panic.

"If he spoke German when agitated, why didn't he write this out in German as he was dying?"

Jeremiah came to stand beside her. "That's a good question," he said after a moment.

35

"I mean, he had to be afraid, in shock, wouldn't it have been more natural to write his dying words in his native language?"

"It would have," Jeremiah said, his voice taking on a darker quality to it.

She glanced up at him. His face had hardened. Moments like this really drove home to her how little she knew of the life he had lived before. He had grown up in Israel where the threat of violence hung forever over his head.

"So, there must be a really important reason he wrote his final word in Hebrew."

"Your logic makes sense. I just don't see what that could be."

"Maybe after you've translated more we'll be able to figure that out."

"We?" he asked, face softening again as he turned to look at her. "Frankly, I was planning on turning over the recorder to Mark and washing my hands of this mess as soon as I was done."

"The man came to you wanting to talk. You can't tell me that you aren't even the least little bit curious," she said.

"Would it help if I told you I wasn't?"

"No, I'd just call you a liar."

"Okay, I admit that I am curious. But that's not enough for me to risk my life or yours any more than I have to."

"And I have had a lifetime of being in danger," she said fervently. "But I really think this is significant, it means something."

"You might be right. Tell you what? Let me finish translating all of this," he said, gesturing around the room, "and then we can talk about what we will or will not do."

"Great," she said. "I'd hate to think of his killer going free if we could do something to catch him."

"Believe it or not, I do understand. It's just that we don't have to be involved this time and I'd love to keep it that way. Plus, this is one of the busiest times of the year for me and I can't shirk my responsibilities to chase after phantoms."

"Really? This is usually one of the slower times for us."

"You don't have five major holidays all happening in the span of about three weeks."

"Five? Five?" she asked incredulously.

"Yes, five," he said, sounding suddenly very tired.

"What are they?"

"Rosh Hashanah starts in three days and at the culmination of it is Yom Kippur. Less than a week later is Sukkot. Then immediately after that is Shmini Atzeret followed by Simchat Torah. And there's also a fast, Tzom Gedaliah, in there."

Cindy stared at him in amazement. "I confess the only two I've even heard of are Rosh Hashanah and Yom Kippur and even those I'm fuzzy on what they're all about."

"I'd be happy to tell you all about them, but if I don't get this done before Rosh Hashanah I'm going to have a big problem."

"I'll take a rain check then," she said.

"It's a deal. Now I have to get back to this. You're welcome to stay, though, if you don't mind listening."

She smiled. "I'd like that. Who knows, maybe I can figure out why this word was so important to him."

"Works for me."

He turned back to the wall and began reading into his recorder again. Cindy listened as she continued to look around the room, trying to see if there was anything else that seemed out of place.

There was nothing, so she finally sat down and continued to listen as Jeremiah read aloud what life had been like for the young man growing up in war torn Germany. He expressed so many emotions, confusion, fear, anger, and then, at the last, hatred.

His family's small brewery was taken over by the government, but even though it was the work of Nazis because of the constant programming and propaganda, he blamed the Jews.

At one point he described beating a Jewish man nearly to death before soldiers took him away to one of the concentration camps. Jeremiah came to a stop and turned off the recorder. She looked at him closely. His face was white and she couldn't tell what he was feeling, she just knew it was terrible.

She stood up and crossed over to him and hesitantly put a hand on his shoulder. He jerked and then looked at her, face strained, eyes wide.

"I'm sorry," she said. "I can see how painful this is. I know what they did to your people."

He looked at her like she was insane and there was such a mixture of fury and bewilderment in his eyes that she actually felt afraid. She took a step backward, dropping her hand.

"You're from Israel. You were born and raised there," she said.

He nodded.

"But yet, the way you've been pronouncing all those German names you sound like a native German speaker. And you said he spoke German to you when he was agitated. You understood him, didn't you?"

Again he nodded.

"Your family, before Israel was created at the end of the war, where were they living?"

"Germany," he whispered.

Tears began to pour down her face. "I am so sorry."

"My mother was born in one of those camps. Both my grandparents died there, but she and her older brother survived."

"I had no idea."

"How could you?" he asked, eyes burning. "I never told you."

Cindy didn't know what to say. Worse, she didn't know what to do. She wanted to hold him, comfort him, but he had looked so fierce when she merely touched him that she was afraid that would be the wrong thing.

He passed a hand over his eyes.

"I need to get some air," he muttered.

"We could go for a walk," she suggested.

He shook his head. "You stay, I'll just be a minute."

As soon as he had left Cindy began to walk through the rest of the downstairs, her agitation making it impossible to sit still.

The emptiness of the place was unnerving, especially when contrasted with all the chaos in her own head. She'd never realized that there was such tragedy in Jeremiah's family, although she should have. It explained a lot.

I'm not the only one whose lost a family member in a horrible way, she realized.

She kept pacing for a few minutes and then she finally went upstairs, driven by curiosity and the need to look at something different than bare walls and floors. Only upstairs it was more of the same. She paced through each room, eyes searching for something the police might have missed, even though she knew it was arrogance on her part to think she'd be the one to find the overlooked clue.

You're getting full of yourself, she chastised.

She went back downstairs finally after exhausting every nook and cranny upstairs.

The only place she hadn't checked out downstairs was the small cubby hole storage area under the stairs. She opened it and walked in. The room sloped down quickly but was bigger than most spaces of its kind.

A memory tugged at her heart. The house they had lived in when she was little had a room like this. Her older sister had commandeered it as her playroom and held fantastic tea parties with her stuffed animals in it.

That was before she died, back when the world was still a safe, wonderful place.

Cindy could feel the tears threatening to come and she pushed them back. Her sister had been gone for so long and yet still she was occasionally ambushed like this by memories.

She was about to leave the space when she decided to go all the way into the corners where the light wasn't falling, just in case there was anything there. Of course, that was incredibly unlikely. Everything else in the place was stripped bare. The old man had probably never even put anything in here.

Still she got down on her hands and knees and crawled in until she could reach her hands into the corners. There was nothing. She shifted her weight slightly and the floor squeaked beneath her. She began to back up and her hand fell on a place on the carpet that seemed off somehow.

She paused and ran her hands over the carpet. There was a section that seemed to be the tiniest bit lower than the rest. That made no sense.

She continued to feel around and she discovered that the section seemed to be nearly the width of the closet but was only about two feet deep, forming a weird rectangle shape.

She felt along the ridge. It was like a seem. She felt a surge of excitement. Could it actually be a trap door of some kind leading to under the house? Was there a basement down there?

Some houses had trap doors into the crawl space beneath a house just like they had doors in the ceiling to enable you to reach into the attic area.

She heard the front door open and close and she scooted out of the closet. Jeremiah came down the hall and stopped. "What are you doing?" he asked.

"I think I found a trap door in here," she said, unable to contain her excitement. "I think it's worth a look."

She showed him where and after running his hands over the area he sat back. "I think you're right," he said.

"Should we call Mark?"

He shook his head. "Odds are there's nothing down there but spiders and dirt. No harm in checking, though."

"I don't feel any kind of ring or anything to lift it with."

"I've got a crowbar in my trunk, let's see if we can find a place to fit it and get this thing open."

Cindy waited impatiently as Jeremiah went to retrieve the tool. When he came back she gave him space to be able to work. After a minute he said, "I think I found a crack. Hold on."

Moments later he was lifting a trapdoor. She had been right.

"We need a flashlight," he said. "I don't have one of those in my car."

"Here, I've got an app on my phone," she said, quickly turning it on.

She moved forward and shone the light from her phone down into the hole. The first thing she saw was a spider web and she almost laughed. Jeremiah had been right about the spiders.

"There's something in here," he said.

"What?"

He propped the trap door open and reached in. He pulled out a long, flat package wrapped in brown paper. He put it down on the ground when he had freed it from its space. One corner of the package had been torn open and there were dark stains covering much of it.

"It looks like a painting of some kind," Jeremiah said.

"Do you think it's valuable?" she breathed, excitement rippling through her.

"I don't know, but we need to call Mark, right now," he said, his voice urgent.

"Why?"

"It's covered in dried blood."

Jeremiah called Mark and the detective was there within fifteen minutes.

"I have to say I knew it would speed things up if I sent her here," Mark said, eyeing Cindy. "I just didn't expect you to find something hidden in the house."

"Is that why you called me?" Cindy asked.

Mark shrugged. "Why fight it, you two are impressive together." He gave Jeremiah a sly smile and it took all of Jeremiah's willpower not to snap his neck.

"I guess we do make a pretty good team," Cindy said.

Mark looked like he was about to make some further comment and Jeremiah glared at him, letting just enough menace show through that the detective actually looked startled. He blinked at Jeremiah for a moment and then turned to Cindy. He pulled a pair of gloves out of his pocket and put them on.

"Show me what you found."

Cindy led the way to the storage closet and Mark crouched as he went inside. Jeremiah could see the detective shining a flashlight around. After a couple of minutes he reemerged carrying the painting. "There doesn't seem to be anything else in there," he said.

He hauled the painting into the room with the lettering because it had the most light and set it on the ground.

"The paper has already been loosened," Jeremiah noted.

Mark nodded and gently peeled back the brown covering.

Both Jeremiah and Cindy leaned forward to get a better look and Jeremiah noted that Cindy was holding her breath. He felt a certain sense of excitement himself, wondering what was worth the trouble of hiding like that.

Finally the detective had the paper pulled back far enough that they could get a decent look at the painting beneath.

They all stared in stunned silence for a moment which Cindy finally broke. "I don't believe it," she said, disappointment heavy in her voice. "It's just that dogs playing poker print that you see everywhere."

"Something seems really off about this," Mark muttered, eyes roving over the painting.

"Why would he go to all the trouble to hide this?" Cindy asked.

"Maybe because of the blood on the wrapping?" Jeremiah suggested.

"Yeah, but why not just dispose of that?" Mark asked. "I swear, this case just keeps getting weirder and weirder." Mark pulled the painting free and flipped it over. The back was smooth with no mounting brackets of any kind.

"This can't be the picture that was hanging in the dining room," Jeremiah said.

"What? What do you mean?" Mark asked with a frown.

"There's a nail hole in the dining room as though a picture or something was hanging in there at one time. There's no hardware on this, so this can't be it."

"Show me," Mark said.

He and Cindy followed Jeremiah into the dining room where he pointed out the nail hole. The detective studied it for a moment and then sighed.

"Just once I'd like a nice straight-forward homicide. Find the killer standing over the body with the smoking gun saying 'yep, I did it'. Is that too much to ask?"

Jeremiah knew it was a rhetorical question, but he still had to bite his tongue to keep from giving a sarcastic reply.

The detective turned with a sigh. "What else have you come up with?"

Jeremiah gave him the condensed version of what he'd been able to translate so far and Mark jotted a few notes down in his notebook.

When he was finished Cindy jumped in. "What have you been able to find out?"

Mark looked at her in surprise. "Oh no, we're not doing that again. I'm the detective, remember?"

"You invited both of us here, so I think we're involved, and this time the only one you can blame is yourself," Cindy said tartly.

Jeremiah noticed that despite her tough words she looked a little flustered and he hid a smile. She had come such a long way from the woman he had first met who was screaming over a dead body in her church sanctuary. She was still uncomfortable, though, with being aggressive. It was actually very endearing.

Mark glared but then gave in a moment later. "You're right, it's my fault. Okay, all I know so far is that the guy appears to have been in this country for decades, but he's never held any kind of job that I can find a record of. He has a checking account with decent money in it, he makes regular deposits in cash, and spends very little. He owns this house outright and has for the past ten years."

"Ten years?" Cindy asked. "He's had this place for ten years? Surely he couldn't have been living in it all this time."

"I can't find a record of him living anywhere else for the past ten years, so I guess so."

"It's like he only ever really used the bedroom and the writing room," Jeremiah said.

"Writing room, funny," Mark said. "I'm sure he used the reading room, too."

Jeremiah looked at him, not understanding what he meant.

"You know, the bath- oh, never mind."

Cindy struggled and failed to hide a grin.

"Okay, I'm going to have the forensic guys check this painting out and the blood on the wrapping," Mark said. "Are you two getting ready to call it a night?"

Jeremiah shook his head. "I'd like to, but like I said, I only have so much time I can devote to this before Rosh Hashanah. I need to keep going if I'm going to have a chance at getting done on time."

"Sorry, I know you must be even more exhausted than I am," Mark said in a rare show of compassion.

"It's alright. It needs to get done," Jeremiah said.

"I'll stay for a while longer and see if I can find any other hiding spots," Cindy said.

"I'd tell you not to bother, but with your luck, there's probably a dozen more dogs playing poker paintings hidden around here and you're the only one who could find them," Mark said.

"I'm guessing that's a compliment?" Cindy said.

"Yeah, I guess it is," Mark said, sounding tired. "Well, kids, call me if you find anything else."

He gathered up the painting and its packaging and left.

As soon as the door had closed behind him Jeremiah turned to Cindy. "You don't have to stay, you know."

"It's okay, I want to," she said with a smile. "I know you're busy, but I missed spending time with you at lunch today. And who knows, maybe there are more hiding places around here. Besides, as soon as I go home Geanie's just going to rope me into helping her make more decisions about the wedding."

"You don't enjoy that?"

Cindy shrugged. "It can be fun sometimes, but also overwhelming and exhausting. I guess if I'm completely honest, too, I have to admit that I'm a tad bit jealous that she's so happy and in love. I mean, I'm really excited and pleased for her and Joseph, it's just I guess..." she trailed off.

"I guess that could be hard," Jeremiah said, feeling a bit unsettled.

"So, bottom line, I'm happy to be here with you hunting for clues. I think I'll head back upstairs and work my way down."

"Okay," Jeremiah said. "Let me know if you need anything."

"Of course," she said brightly. She rested her hand on his arm for just a moment and then she moved past him heading for the stairs at the front of the house. He turned and watched her go and found himself wishing inexplicably that she wasn't leaving, even if it was just to go upstairs.

He shook himself and returned to the wall he was translating. He felt his chest tighten slightly. He didn't like the section he'd just read and he was concerned about what was probably coming next. Still, there was no one else who could do it and it had to be done. He found his spot, turned on his recorder and picked up translating where he'd left off.

"Hurting the man made me to feel powerful and lessened my impotence for everything else with my family and our property. I thought this a sign and that if I hurt one man and felt this then if I hurt more it would take all the pain."

Jeremiah paused, squeezing his eyes shut. Yes, the narrative was going exactly as he had feared it was going to go. A young, angry, disempowered boy in Hitler's Germany. There was only one logical way this was going to end.

Heinrich went on to detail every act of cruelty he had perpetrated with excruciating detail. Jeremiah finally had to pause to gather himself and to do some serious thinking. Mark would be listening to this recording, his retelling of these atrocities. He had to decide exactly what emotions he should be correctly displaying and make sure that his voice reflected those.

While he was thinking about it he heard Cindy walking down the stairs. A moment later she came into the room he was in and he welcomed the reprieve.

"Find anything?" he asked.

"No," she said, clearly disappointed.

"Well, maybe something more will turn up down here."

"I found the door that leads to the attic crawlspace in the ceiling of one of the closets, but I have no way to get up there," she said, eyeing his ladder.

"Tell you what, when I'm finished here for the night, I'll take the ladder upstairs and check it out. Deal?"

"Deal," she said, looking happier.

"So, how was your day before all this?" he asked.

She rolled her eyes. "My mom called this morning to share more of my brother's exploits."

"What's Kyle up to this time?"

"He just signed a contract for some new television series. More daredevil globe-trotting stuff I'm sure."

"One of these days I'm going to have to meet him," Jeremiah said.

"It's amazing how different the two of us are," she said.

That might have once been true, but it was changing. She just didn't realize it. He thought about pointing out how much more daring she'd become, but decided against it.

"Your mom say anything else?"

"No, just about Kyle, as usual. You know, she never even asks about the murders we solve or how things are going with you or Geanie or anything."

"I'm sorry," Jeremiah said, knowing that Cindy wished for more validation from her parents.

"What about your mom?" she asked suddenly.

"What about her?"

"What does she have to say about our adventures?" she asked.

Jeremiah forced a smile. "She thinks they are unbelievable and that you are either the luckiest or the unluckiest woman in America. She can't make up her mind."

Cindy laughed. "Some days neither can I."

It was a lie, but he couldn't tell her the truth, it would raise too many questions he wasn't willing to answer. He had never told his mother about her because he didn't talk to his mother, couldn't, not ever, nor any of the rest of the family. Cindy lived in a world, though, where such a thing would be unthinkable. She would ask questions that he never wanted her to ask and then...

He didn't want to think about what would happen then. So he just kept smiling at her, pretending that everything was normal, that *he* was normal. Which was in its own way ludicrous given that they were standing in a dead man's house searching for hidden art and translating his ramblings about torturing Jews during World War II.

Normal was relative.

"Things were interesting at work, too," Cindy said after a minute.

"Oh?"

"Dave threatened to quit."

"Wildman?" Jeremiah asked, surprised. "What happened?"

"The head pastor and the music director are at each other's throats again and they both dragged him into it."

"That's a shame," Jeremiah said. Fights like that could tear organizations apart, churches being no exception. "Well, if anyone needs a good counselor," he joked.

She rolled her eyes. "Don't tease. I might make you come in and facilitate."

He chuckled. "Now that would be funny."

Cindy glanced at her watch. "It's getting late."

"I need to get a little more done," he said, wishing that weren't the case.

She looked torn. Finally he suggested, "Why don't you go home and get some rest? I'm going to be here all day tomorrow and you can look at it all with fresh eyes then."

She nodded. "Do you want me to swing by and take Captain out for a walk?" Captain was Jeremiah's German Shepherd who he'd had for the better part of a year now.

"No, I asked Marie to walk him on her way home. Thanks, though."

"Okay. If you're sure," she said, still hesitating even as she grabbed her purse.

"Completely. One of us should get some rest."

"Okay. I'll see you tomorrow."

After she left he noticed that the empty house seemed so much colder. He grabbed the digital recorder and went back to work.

Cindy hated leaving Jeremiah alone in the dead man's house, but she was exhausted and knew he was right that she'd be able to do a better job of searching the next day. She wished she didn't have to go to work so she could head over right after breakfast and continue the search.

In the back of her mind she knew that she was jumping into this case with an eagerness that was new and uncharacteristic. Usually she was dragged into these things kicking and screaming but this time she had marched in cheerfully.

It had to be because Mark had already involved Jeremiah. It wasn't right to make him go through this by himself. If Jeremiah hadn't been involved she probably wouldn't have even given a thought to getting involved. Of course, Mark never would have called her and she wouldn't even have known there was something to get involved in.

When she made it home she found Geanie and Joseph snuggled up on the couch watching a movie. Geanie turned off the television and practically pounced on her. "What happened? You were gone longer than just dinner."

"I kind of got involved searching the house for clues," Cindy admitted.

"And?" Geanie asked, eyes wide.

"I found one," Cindy said, feeling the thrill of discovery anew as she got to share. "Of course, it ended up being really weird."

"Don't leave us in suspense," Joseph said.

Cindy smiled. Over the last year-and-a-half Joseph had become a really good friend. It really was weird. Before finding the body in the church she'd had no close friends at all and now she had three of them.

I guess it's true that adversity can really bring people closer together.

"Well, I found a painting hidden under a trap door in a closet under the stairs. There was blood on the packaging."

"No!" Geanie said.

"Yes," Cindy answered, delighted to have such an enthusiastic audience.

"Was it valuable?" Joseph asked.

"Hardly. It just turned out to be one of those prints of the dogs playing poker."

"Why was it hidden?" Geanie asked.

"No idea."

"Whose blood was it?" Joseph asked.

"Mark is having forensics try to figure that out. Hopefully we'll know more soon."

"I can't believe you're involved in another mystery," Geanie said. "You didn't even get sucked into this one either."

"Which as far as I'm concerned begs the question of whether this is about solving the mystery or spending even more time with the guy?" Joseph said.

Cindy felt herself flush. "Trust me, Joseph, if I had feelings for anyone in that way, you'd be the first to know."

"So you say," he said with a smile.

It was probably true. She had been the first person Joseph had told that he was planning to propose to Geanie several months before. Odds were good she'd end up confiding those types of things in him even before she confided them to Geanie.

But there was nothing to confide. *Absolutely nothing*, she told herself.

"So, what are you guys watching?" she asked.

"A clever ruse to change the subject," Geanie noted.

Cindy rolled her eyes. Geanie was right back to center, seeing love in all the wrong places.

"Okay, let's not tease," Joseph said, squeezing Geanie's shoulders. "We were watching one of Geanie's weird horror movies that she loves.

"Weird?" Geanie asked in mock outrage. "You want to talk about weird?"

"No, not really," Joseph said with a cherubic smile.

Cindy couldn't help but laugh. The two of them were an adorable couple.

"You want to join us?" Joseph asked.

"Sure, I haven't been subjected to one of her weird horror films in like two weeks," Cindy said.

"I'll grab you some popcorn," Geanie said.

"But I was told it's bad form to throw it at the screen," Joseph said straight-faced.

Cindy started laughing harder. It felt so good. She remembered her life before when she'd never really laughed much. It had been such a sad life, even if it was safe. Then, after what had happened to her over Memorial Day weekend, she'd worried she'd never be able to laugh and relax again. She shouldn't have feared. She still had nightmares and still got jittery from time-to-time, but with Geanie and Joseph around, it was impossible to stay freaked out for too long.

"Better explain to her what a Triffid is," Joseph said.

"No need, we can just start from the beginning," Geanie said brightly.

Joseph groaned.

Cindy joined them on the couch and let herself be taken away by the cheesy film. A part of her mind still couldn't stop thinking about Jeremiah, the ink covered walls, and the painting. She almost felt like she was two people, one laughing and cringing at the television and one furiously working on solving the most challenging puzzle she'd ever encountered. It was a bit surreal, which strangely fit with the movie they were trying to watch.

They were just reaching the climax of the film when the house phone rang shrilly and made all three of them jump.

Cindy got up and grabbed it, glancing at the clock as she did so. It was too late for anyone she knew to be calling. A knife twisted in her stomach, wondering if something had happened to someone.

"Hello?" she asked, hearing her voice shake.

"Cindy, it's Jeremiah," he said, his voice hushed.

"What's wrong?" she asked, heart beginning to race.

"Get over here right n-"

The call disconnected.

"Jeremiah!" Cindy shouted, but he was gone. She dialed with shaking hands but it went straight to his voicemail. She grabbed her purse and keys.

"What's wrong?" Geanie asked, starting up from the couch.

"Something's happened to Jeremiah," Cindy shouted on her way to the door.

She heard Geanie yelling something after her, but she didn't know what. She yanked her phone out of her purse and saw that she'd missed a call from him right before he'd called her house. He hadn't left a message.

She called Mark and was reversing her car down the driveway when he picked up.

"Jeremiah called me," she began.

"I know, I'm on my way over there," he said. "I'll call once I know what's going on."

He hung up and she screamed in frustration as she threw her phone into the passenger seat. She drove as fast as she dared and nearly ran a red light before she realized there was too much traffic. When she finally pulled up outside the house and saw Mark's car as well as several others her heart sank.

She stopped in the middle of the street and ran to the house abandoning her car, her purse, everything. She got tangled in the police line tape and sobbed in frustration until one end ripped free and she was able to make it into the house. She searched for a face she recognized as she kept running farther into the house.

She made it into the writing room and came to a stop. There was Jeremiah, seemingly unharmed, talking intently with Mark. She leaped over to them.

"I got here as soon as I could, are you okay?"

"I'm fine. I wanted you to see what I found before they took it away and my cell phone died on me," Jeremiah said.

She blinked at him. "You weren't in any danger."

"No, I'm sorry, did you think-"

She felt woozy, like she was going to be sick or pass out. As one in a dream she saw herself raising her hand and she slapped Jeremiah across the face. "How could you do that to me! I thought you were attacked!" she heard herself shouting.

Hands were grabbing her shoulders and she was vaguely aware that they were Mark's.

Jeremiah stared at her, a look of complete shock on his face. He slowly lifted his hand to his cheek where a bright red handprint was emblazoned. She could hear herself sobbing, but it sounded like somebody else far away. Her cheeks felt wet and she tasted salt on her lips.

She was being pulled away and she didn't want to go, but something told her that she should. Mark was whispering something to her, or maybe he was shouting, she couldn't tell, but he was steering her toward the front door.

Outside there was a light breeze that fanned her cheeks. There was a roaring sound in her ears and the corners of her vision were going black. She felt pressure downward on her shoulders and she let Mark push her down to a seat on the curb.

Then he pressed against the back of her head until she realized that she had her head between her knees. She still felt sick, but slowly the roaring in her ears eased up. She squeezed her eyes shut and realized she was crying.

And then she heard Mark distinctly say, "Are you any better?"

"I guess not," she whispered. She'd thought the stress of what had happened to her and Jeremiah in Hawaii had faded into the background and that she had mostly recovered from the experience. But in one moment she had been right back there and all the feelings of terror and helplessness had come racing back. She had thought for sure that Jeremiah had survived drowning then only to be killed by someone now.

"I get that, but you can hear me now?"

She nodded.

He put his hand on her back and rubbed it gently up and down. "You feel like you're going to pass out still?"

"I'm not sure, I don't think so. How did you know that's what was happening?"

"I've seen it before," he said.

She should lift her head and talk to him, but she kept it between her knees with her eyes tightly shut. She no longer felt like she was going to pass out, but she still felt terrible and she didn't know what to do about it.

"It's okay. It's called Posttraumatic Stress Disorder."

"But I've been doing so well."

"PTSD shows up in many people about three months away from the event that caused it but sometimes can start years later even. I'd say you're about right on schedule. You know, I could recommend a really good counselor, but unfortunately he's the guy you just slapped."

"Are you actually teasing me?" she asked.

"Only a little. I will admit, I'll treasure the look on his face for years to come. I've almost hit him myself more times than I can count."

She finally looked up. Mark was smiling gently at her, but it was a compassionate smile.

"I know after I was kidnapped, your wife Traci said that if I ever needed to talk about it, I could talk with her."

"And she would be happy to talk to you about her own experiences after she was kidnapped. She can certainly relate better than I or your roommate or that guy in there can."

Cindy nodded. "Maybe I'll ask her out to lunch."

"I'd say that would be a good first step. You want to talk to a doctor or a therapist, or whomever, you let me know and I'll find you the best."

"Thanks, I appreciate it," she said.

"You're going to get through this."

She nodded. "I just...that all came out of nowhere."

Mark tilted his head to the side. "Not really. It was the first time you thought you were facing a threat to someone you care about since everything happened. Until you encountered a situation where you felt that type of fear there was no telling how you'd react. But, frankly, that's about what I would have expected. For my part, I'm sorry. I didn't realize his phone cut out before he could explain things to you. I was trying to steer around a group of pedestrians and had to get off the phone fast.

Had I realized what you were thinking I would have told you everything was okay."

"It's not your fault," she said.

"No, but I'm still going to buy you a milkshake or whatever you drink so I feel better about it."

"Now you are teasing me," she accused.

"Yes."

"Then you do owe me a milkshake."

"Fair enough. So, how are you feeling now?" he asked.

"Better. Really embarrassed."

"Don't be. We've all been there or at least seen someone who has. No one here is going to hold that against you. In fact," he said, lowering his voice conspiratorially. "I'm betting everyone inside wishes they had gotten to slap him instead."

"I have a hard time believing that."

"Believe it. They were all here earlier and they're pretty irritated that they didn't find what he did."

Cindy wiped her eyes. Her curiosity started to rear its head. "Okay, what is it he found."

Mark gave her a huge grin. "Trust me, you'll have to see it to believe it. When you're ready, I'll take you inside and show you."

"Can you at least give me a hint?"

"Oh, okay," he said, sounding like a parent caving in to the demands of an eager child. "Well, let's see. I can tell you how he found what he did."

"Okay."

"As he told it, he was just finishing up for the night. He went into the master bedroom to use the master bathroom."

"You mean the reading room?" she asked.

"See! You are feeling better," Mark said.

"I'm trying to," she admitted. Making the joke at least helped make her feel a little more human, a little more normal. Then again, she was a fine one to talk about normal. She never had been normal, not since her sister...she shook her head, refusing to let herself go there.

"Okay, so he was heading for the reading room to splash some cold water on his face."

"Not to read then?" she asked weakly.

"Excellent, keep them coming. No, at least, that's his story. He was busy thinking about everything he had just read when he noticed that there was an odd bump in the carpet in the bedroom, just a small one, but he could tell it was there."

"I didn't get to really search that room well after finding the painting," she said.

"If you had, you might have been the one to find it," Mark said. "Of course, none of us would have even thought twice about a bump, small as it was, before you found that trapdoor. Next he notices that the carpet pad seems to be much thicker than in the rest of the house, more cushiony."

"Okay."

"So, he was thinking about the painting that you found, obviously and he just kept staring at that tiny bump and sort of bouncing up and down feeling the cushion and he decided that just maybe there was something hidden under the carpet."

"Was there?"

Mark smiled. "Wait for it. So, he got down on the floor and he started checking all the edges, looking for one that might be loose."

"Because he doesn't want to rip up the carpet if he's wrong?"

"You guessed it."

"Well, back behind the bed he actually found a section that was loose. He was able to pull it up just a tiny bit."

"And?"

"And what he found made him rip half the carpet out anyway before he called me and then you."

She stared at him in anticipation. "And that was?"

He wagged his finger under her nose. "Nope, I told you, you have to see it to believe it. He wouldn't tell me when he called me and now I know why. I wouldn't have truly gotten the...scope...of it. Either that or I would have decided he was hallucinating and told him to go get some sleep."

"You have to tell me."

"I don't have to do anything. But, when you're ready to stand up, I'll take you in there to see it just like I promised."

Cindy took a deep breath. "I'm ready," she said.

She wasn't, but then she couldn't imagine ever being ready to go inside and face the music. She was still trying to wrap her head around exactly what had happened. She didn't know how she'd even begin to apologize to Jeremiah let alone look at all the officers who'd just seen her meltdown. She needed to get it over with, though, and she did really want to see whatever it was that had caused all of this in the first place.

She took another deep breath, bowed her head, and prayed that God would give her the strength to do what she had to. When she finally lifted her head Mark said, "Amen."

She glanced at him in surprise. She knew he wasn't religious.

He shrugged. "I figured that's what you were doing. Was I wrong?"

"No, you weren't."

"Okay then, stop looking at me like I'm crazy then." He stood up and offered her his hands.

She took both of them and felt a bit ashamed that he had to exert more effort to get her on her feet than she did. Once up she wobbled for a moment, her legs weak feeling and she leaned against him.

"It's okay," he said, putting an arm around her. "I'll be right here and I'll help you get through it."

"I'm not used to you being this nice," she said, then realized that was a terrible thing to have admitted.

He grunted. "Take a picture, it will last longer."

"That sounds more like you. I'm sorry, I feel like I've lost my edit chip somehow."

"It's the stress, it's keeping you from being able to filter your thoughts and actions as well. It's okay. You're usually so nice and proper it will be refreshing to have you be a little cruder. Maybe I'll get some curse words out of you before the night is over."

"Don't hold your breath."

He laughed. "See, you will be okay."

She hoped he was right. Together they walked back into the house. The officers that glanced at her looked sympathetic which was better than judgmental but was somehow still hard to take. It made her that much more aware that there was something wrong with her.

And everyone here knows it.

Jeremiah was in the writing room talking with a uniformed officer whose nametag said Liam. She winced when she saw that Jeremiah's cheek was still red where she had struck him.

Jeremiah turned, saw her, and started toward her. When he was in front of her he started to reach out then checked himself and looked at Mark.

"It's okay, you can touch her, she's not going to break," Mark said.

Jeremiah nodded and reached out and hugged her.

She leaned into his chest and fought against starting to cry all over again.

"It's okay," she heard him whisper.

She wrapped her arms around his waist and felt herself shudder. "I thought something had happened to you."

"I'm so sorry I scared you."

She nodded, unable to say anything else around the lump in her throat.

"I'll give you two a minute and then I want to show Cindy what you found," Mark said.

Cindy couldn't help but think that Mark was crazy. It was going to take more than a minute for her to be even remotely okay enough to be able to stand on her own.

Jeremiah locked eyes with Mark and the detective nodded before heading toward the master bedroom. He returned his attention to Cindy. She had her head buried in his chest and he was holding her up. He would gladly hold her up all night if it would help her.

His heart was breaking for her. He had been a fool not to see this coming. Mark hadn't seemed at all surprised. Then again, he saw people living through horrific situations all the time. Most of Jeremiah's counseling duties had nothing to do with helping people survive the kind of horror Cindy had lived through.

"We're going to get through this," he reassured her.

He felt a slight motion, he hoped it was a nod. He rested his chin on the top of her head and closed his eyes, wishing he could take the pain away. He felt a surge of guilt, but he had to remind himself that he hadn't brought this nightmare on her. What had happened to her in Hawaii wasn't his fault and could have, probably would have, happened even if she had never met him.

All he could do was be there for her, be kind and listen and help her get through this.

"It's going to be okay, I promise."

This time he knew she nodded her head which relieved him a little bit.

Around them the police officers continued to do their jobs. Finally after another minute he felt Cindy begin to straighten. He let her push away from him when she was ready.

Her eyes were red and puffy and he fought the urge to wipe the tears from her cheeks. He would do anything to wipe the haunted look from her eyes and to make her smile again. She stared at him, so vulnerable, so raw, and he couldn't stand it. He needed to make it better.

He started to lean down toward her and then froze as he realized what he had been about to do. She didn't seem to realize, just kept staring at him with that same lost look. He could feel panic creeping over him and for the first time in a very long time he had absolutely no idea what to do.

"You're looking better," Mark said.

Jeremiah flinched and Cindy turned away to face Mark, dashing away the tears from under her eyes.

"I am doing a bit better," she said.

Her voice sounded stronger.

But Jeremiah had lost his.

Her legs were steady and holding her up on their own now.

His were about to collapse.

She was putting on a brave face, struggling to pretend, to make everything okay.

Jeremiah was certain he would never be okay ever again.

"So, are you ready to see what the rabbi found?" Mark asked cheerfully.

"Yes, I'm ready," she said.

"Come with me."

Mark turned and left the room. Cindy followed him.

Jeremiah was rooted to the ground but his eyes followed until she was lost to sight.

His entire world was collapsing around him. And she didn't even know. She didn't realize what had just happened. She had no clue how near she had come to disaster.

But Jeremiah knew. And he knew everything that it would have meant. He needed space. He needed to leave the house and get away from everyone and everything. He needed to be able to center himself until he had control over his own actions again. He needed this because he knew what Cindy did not.

Jeremiah had been about to kiss her.

6

Officers were carrying furniture out of the bedroom and Mark gestured for Cindy to wait a moment while they finished. She leaned against the wall and a minute later they carried carpet and padding out.

"Okay, wait until you see this," Mark said, a huge grin on his face that she could tell was completely genuine. Whatever it was he was truly excited for her to see it.

She stepped forward, looked into the room and then just stared, slack-jawed, struggling to comprehend what she was seeing.

"I know, right?" Mark said.

The entire floor looked like it was made of gold with ornate carvings toward the edges and semi-precious stones scattered throughout. Light from the ceiling was reflected all along the surface and it almost seemed to shimmer.

"It's beautiful," she whispered.

"I know."

"Is it gold?" she asked.

"It looks like it, but the theory is that it's actually amber."

"Really?"

"Yeah, the rabbi has a theory that this is a piece of the Amber Room."

"What's the Amber Room?" Cindy asked. She felt like she'd heard the name once a longtime ago, it had a vague familiarity to it in that way, but she didn't know anything beyond that.

"It was a cultural treasure plundered by the Nazis when they invaded Russia," Jeremiah said behind her.

She jumped slightly, startled to realize he was standing behind her and she hadn't known it.

"Really?" she asked.

"Yes, they stole it from the Catherine Palace in Pushkin. The room, made out of amber and completed with jewels was originally a gift to Peter the Great to celebrate peace between Russia and Prussia in 1716. It's one of the most famous art treasures looted during the war that's never been recovered."

"That's amazing, but what's a piece of it doing here?" Cindy breathed, unable to take her eyes off of it.

"That would be the million dollar question," Mark said.

Cindy continued to stare at it for another minute and then asked. "What are you going to do with it?"

"We need to box it up and send it to a lab for testing and authentication if that's possible," Mark said. "We can't leave it here."

She nodded, feeling disappointed that she wouldn't be able to see it again. It was a truly magnificent sight and for a just a few moments it had made her forget about everything else.

"Okay, time for you to go home and get some rest while we take care of this," Mark said at last.

She nodded, grateful that Jeremiah had called her to come see this despite what had happened because of it.

Mark had gotten a late start in the morning, oversleeping his alarm. In the old days Paul would have called him and woke him up. Sometimes it was the simple things about having a partner that he missed. As it was Traci woke him up to let him know that she would be having lunch with Cindy. He was hoping it would do them both some good. Traci had been through so much in the last year it would do her good to talk to somebody other than him and he was sure that she'd be able to help Cindy a great deal as well.

He made it into the station and sat down at his desk. He'd had four cups of coffee so far and he still felt like something the cat had dragged in. He wiped a hand across his eyes as he tried to get himself to focus.

"Come on, you can pull it together," he encouraged himself.

There were a couple of phone messages for him, nothing that seemed urgent, but he figured he'd get them out of the way first. He'd just hung up from the last one when Liam stopped by his desk.

"You're out of uniform," Mark noticed. He hadn't meant it to sound critical, he was just commenting on what he was seeing, but still Liam looked flustered.

"It's my day off," the officer explained.

"Then why are you here? Don't you have somewhere better to be? Someone to be with?"

"My girlfriend is working until five and I was up late thinking about some stuff."

Mark wasn't sure where this was heading, but he knew for a fact that he was too tired to deal with it, whatever it was.

Liam had an envelope in his hand and Mark pointed to it. "What's that?"

Liam handed it over. "This just came for you."

"Unless it's a signed confession by the killer or a map showing the location of Jimmy Hoffa's body, I'm not interested."

Liam's eyes widened and Mark felt bad. With a sigh he took the envelope and tore it open. Inside was an art auction catalogue. He dropped it on his desk in disgust.

Liam glanced at it. "I didn't take you as an art collector."

"I'm not," Mark snapped. "It's just a little dig from an art dealer's relatives to remind me that even though he was killed about a year ago we still haven't caught whoever was responsible."

"I don't understand," Liam confessed.

"Tell you what? It's your day off, let's go get some coffee. I'll tell you about this and you'll tell me whatever it is you've been thinking about."

There was a coffee shop across the street from the station. He and Paul had always gone there because strangely none of the other cops did. He and Liam walked across and it amused him that the younger cop insisted they use the crosswalk.

"You'd honestly ticket someone for jaywalking?"

"Yes, I would," Liam said.

"You'd ticket a cop for jaywalking?"

"Absolutely."

They ordered their coffee and sat down at a table in the corner.

"You're that much of a stickler for the rules?" Mark asked, unwilling to drop it.

"It's my job to be," Liam answered simply.

"Then maybe you can answer a question for me," Mark said.

"I'll certainly try."

"How come you're the only guy in this precinct that will look me in the eyes?"

Liam blinked at him, clearly taken aback by the question. "I-I don't understand," he said.

"Sure you do. I screwed up big time back in March. Everyone's still treating me like a leper because of that, but not you. And yet I find out you're more hardnosed about the rules than anyone else at the station."

"It's my job to uphold the law. It's not my job to judge people," Liam said after a minute. "Everyone breaks the law at some point, even if it's just running a stop sign. I know what you did and I know you've suffered because of it. I also know that they let you back on the force. It's not my job to decide punishment. If I wanted to do that I would have become a lawyer in the hopes of being a judge some day."

It was Mark's turn to be surprised. "That's very enlightened of you," he said at last.

Liam shrugged. "It's how I see it. Now will you tell me what you meant about the art auction?"

"Okay," Mark said, leaning back in his chair. "About a year ago a local art dealer by the name of Mike Haverston was killed in the storage room at his store. My partner and I worked every angle we could for a month but could never catch a break. Let's just say his kids were less than pleased with our lack of progress. I know they finished probating the will recently, so now it looks like they're selling off all their father's stuff. I think they sent me the catalogue as a dig reminding me that I failed their father and them by not catching his killer."

"As insults go, an auction catalogue is pretty subtle," Liam noted.

"Yeah, well all of them were pretty snooty and the slightest snub or rude comment was a huge deal in their world. Anyway, it was one of the few cases my partner and I were never able to close."

"I'm sorry, I know that must be frustrating."

Mark shrugged. "It is what it is, but then again, I've been getting more used to letting people down lately."

Liam looked like he wanted to argue that point so Mark changed the subject. "So, what did you spend last night thinking about?"

"I looked it up and there are still hundreds of thousands of pieces of art missing from World War II."

Mark shook his head and whistled. "Wow, that's a staggering amount of art."

"And a staggering amount of money. Most of the really famous pieces have been found. The last one to be discovered not that long ago was Raphael's painting Portrait of a Young Man. It was found in a bank vault somewhere."

"That's probably where a lot of that stuff is," Mark said.

"Maybe, but the Nazis buried a lot of the art and other valuables that they stole in caves, mines, old breweries. A lot of people think there's still several caches that have gone undiscovered."

Mark leaned forward. "Did you say breweries?"

"Yes."

"Heinrich's parents had a small brewery."

"Yes. When the Amber Room was stolen in Russia they disassembled it and packed it into 47 large crates. If what we found in his house really is part of it, it's a very tiny part."

"And Heinrich might have known where the rest of it was," Mark said. "And if anyone else guessed his secret that would be worth killing for."

"Exactly what I was thinking."

Mark shook his head. "It's a good story, but it's still wild speculation at this point. I mean, what are the odds that what we recovered from that house is actually a piece of the real Amber Room? They have to be astronomical."

"It's a long way from where it was last seen to California, but it's not impossible," Liam said.

"But if Heinrich actually had this thing, why hide it? Why not go public or sell it on the black market and cash in?"

"Maybe he was trying to and that's what got him killed."

Mark rolled his neck, trying to relax the muscles. "We'll know a lot more when the lab guys come back with information on everything we found yesterday."

Waiting on the lab's analysis, waiting on Jeremiah's translation. It seemed like there was nothing he was going to be able to do except wait.

He hated waiting.

Cindy had seriously contemplated calling in and taking a mental health day. Clearly if there was anyone in need of restoring their mental health it was her. Ultimately, though, she decided against it even though she had had very little sleep. Doing something nice and calm and normal, sticking with her routine, was what she probably needed. She had called Marks' wife, Traci, on the way in to work and had arranged to meet her for lunch just like she'd promised Mark the night before.

The office had been blessedly quiet all morning. She left a couple of minutes early for lunch and drove to Rigatoni's, a small Italian restaurant downtown that she loved.

She walked inside and Traci waved from a table across the room. Cindy headed over and sat down across from her.

"Thanks for meeting me," she said.

"I was glad to do it," Traci said, reaching over and patting her hand.

Even though she felt awkward Cindy knew this was a good idea. If anyone could relate to what she was going through it was Traci who herself had been kidnapped almost a year before.

The waitress came and Cindy ordered the chicken fettuccine alfredo like she usually did.

"So, how have you been?" Traci asked once the waitress had left.

Cindy grimaced. "I'm guessing Mark told you about what happened last night."

Traci nodded. "Believe me, it's completely understandable."

"Have you experienced something like that?" Cindy asked.

"No, but I'm really lucky," Traci said. "Then again, my ordeal was so much shorter than yours, thanks mostly to you. I know Mark kept expecting me to get PTSD. I could still. Some people don't get it until years afterward. I will tell you, though, that I have nightmares like most people couldn't believe."

"You still have them?" Cindy asked.

"At least twice a week. Mark has to wake me up sometimes because I'm screaming and kicking him."

"Ouch."

"Yeah, well, between you and me I think he needs to be kicked every once in a while," Traci said with a sly smile.

Cindy couldn't help but laugh at that. "You're probably right."

"I am, but don't you dare tell him I said that."

"I won't."

"Of course, the same can probably be said of most men."

Cindy thought of her brother, Kyle, whose picture she had routinely thrown darts at for years. "Yeah, my brother could use a good, swift kick somewhere," she muttered.

"Kyle, the one on TV?"

"Yeah, you know him?" Cindy asked.

"I've seen some of his shows," Traci admitted. "He's a real daredevil. I saw the one where he went over the waterfall in a rubber raft."

"I thought I was going to strangle him when he did that. I hate that he takes such chances," Cindy admitted.

"Some people are just like that I guess. It's like they think they're invincible. When I met Mark in college he was kind of that way."

"What happened?"

"He became a cop. He saw firsthand that nobody is invincible," Traci said. "It mellowed him out considerably and made him easier to live with in the process."

"I don't think that anything could mellow my brother out," Cindy said.

Traci shrugged. "Who knows? Maybe someday something or someone will. Until then I'm sure he's happy making millions of people happy."

The waitress dropped off their drinks and some garlic bread.

"I don't get why people love Kyle's shows so much," Cindy lamented once the woman had left.

"It's the purest form of escapism there is," Traci said. "Most of the people who watch his shows lead very structured, boring lives. They're trying to live vicariously through him."

"I guess."

Traci smiled. "Trust me, I know, my family are all huge fans."

"You're kidding me."

"No. In fact when you saved me from the kidnappers I made sure all of them knew that it was Kyle's sister who saved me just so they would be even more impressed."

Normally that would have aggravated Cindy further, but somehow she just found it funny. "I didn't take you for the name dropping type."

Traci rolled her eyes. "With my family if you have a name you have to drop it. That's the only way to shake them up and get their attention. My older sister saw Chuck Norris in an airport once and she led every conversation with that for two months. Anything and everything you could possibly say somehow reminded her of seeing Chuck Norris."

Cindy laughed. "Well, what do you expect? It's Chuck Norris. He can do anything, including giving your sister a good story. I'm just surprised she didn't say something like 'Chuck Norris doesn't fly in planes, he flies next to them.'"

"That's a good one," Traci said. "Or how about Chuck Norris doesn't fly in planes, he flies by himself and carries the plane on his back."

"I love it."

"I'd tell Amber, but I don't want to hear her repeat it a thousand times in the next few weeks."

"You called Amber your older sister. Do you have a younger one?" Cindy asked as she took a bite of garlic bread.

Traci's expression changed. Her skin tightened up and she looked colder, more distant. Cindy knew instantly that she'd accidentally hit a nerve. She could relate. For years she had freaked out any time someone had mentioned her sister.

"I'm sorry, you don't have to talk about it if you don't want to."

"No, it's fine. It's just...Lizzie and I have never been that close. She's twelve years younger than I am and I left for college when she was still little. We ended up having a fight last Christmas which didn't do anything to improve the relationship."

"I'm sorry," Cindy said.

"Yeah. She's always been into trying new things and I'm really not happy with some of her recent choices."

"You want to talk about it?" Cindy asked.

Traci gave her a strained smile. "We're here to talk about you, remember?"

"Yeah, but they don't have to be mutually exclusive."

Traci nodded. "She started playing around with Wicca a couple of years ago. I was okay with it, I mean, it seems like a lot of college girls go through that phase. We grew up in a house without any sort of religion so I got that she was curious and wanted to experiment."

"But something changed?" Cindy guessed.

"Yeah. She used to sound more like a hippie than anything else, you know, 'Respect Mother Earth', 'You get back what you put out into the universe', 'Love all the creatures and respect that bug by not squashing it.' Then, when I saw her at Christmas she was definitely not hippie-esque. She was dark, moody, talked more about spells and power. She even bragged about putting a curse on her ex-boyfriend."

Cindy's stomach tightened. "That's not good," she muttered.

"No, and I told her so. The argument escalated and I don't know what would have happened if Amber hadn't stepped in."

"Did she mention Chuck Norris?" Cindy asked, trying to bring a little levity.

Traci laughed. "Actually she did! She reminded us about seeing him in an airport and was about to tell us how he would handle conflict resolution. Lizzie just stormed out of the house at that point. She came back later, but we didn't talk."

"I'm sorry."

"Thanks. I'm just worried about her at this point, you know? I've called her a couple of times, made sure to let her know that she could talk to me if she wanted to."

"Then you've done what you could."

"I guess," Traci said, looking miserable. "I just wish there was more that I could do."

"If you want I'd be happy to add her to my prayer list."

"You'd do that?" Traci asked, looking surprised.

"Sure, I'd be happy to," Cindy said. "It sounds like she could use some prayer. Actually it sounds like you both could."

"I'd appreciate it," Traci said, wiping at her eyes. She laughed nervously. "That's the first time someone's ever offered to pray for me."

"Really?" Cindy asked, taken aback by the thought.

"Really. It's very sweet. I appreciate it."

Several replies popped into Cindy's head, but she opted to go with the simplest one. "You're welcome," she said with as much compassion as she could put into her voice.

Traci laughed again and picked up her napkin to wipe her eyes. "Okay, enough about me and my crazy sister."

"And my crazy brother," Cindy said with a grin.

Traci picked up her water glass. "A toast."

Cindy picked up her soda glass.

"To my crazy sister and your crazy brother. May they never meet."

"I'll drink to that," Cindy said, clinking glasses with her.

They continued talking, but lunch was over far too soon. As Cindy left and drove back to the church she prayed for Traci and her sister, Lizzie. She couldn't help but feel sorrow for both of them.

As she pulled into the church parking lot she glanced over at the synagogue. She wondered how Jeremiah was doing with the translation. She still felt terrible about hitting him and a little nervous to see him again because of it. She was just going to have to get over that, though. She planned to join him at the house after work and bring dinner again.

She parked, stepped out of her car, and froze. Something didn't feel right to her. She turned around, eyes sweeping over the few cars that were in the parking lot. She saw the normal cars there that staff members drove and a couple of other cars that she recognized that belonged to some of the ministry leaders and volunteers.

There, in the back of the parking lot, was a dark car with tinted windows that she didn't recognize. She knew it hadn't been there when she left for lunch. She stared at it, wondering why someone had parked as far away from the church building as they could. The hair on the back of her neck stood on end and she felt the urge to get back in her car, lock the doors, and drive away quickly.

She took a deep breath, trying to calm herself down. This had to just be paranoia. It was the PTSD rearing its head.

There is nothing wrong or sinister about that car, she thought.

She didn't believe herself.

She was parked right up next to the building. It was only a few steps toward the entrance. She couldn't just stand there in the parking lot all day and leaving was ridiculous.

She took a step toward the entrance, then another, feeling panicky as she left the safety of her car behind.

She was almost at the entrance when she heard an engine rev. She twisted around and saw the car driving toward her. She tensed, getting ready to flee, but it turned and headed for the exit. A moment later it was gone.

"You're being ridiculous," she whispered.

She headed through the gate area and was soon walking past the sanctuary. She could hear people talking inside. Across the way she saw someone walking into the gym. She walked up to the office door. She could hear laughter coming from one of the classrooms across the way.

You see, everything is perfectly normal here, there's nothing to get upset about.

A piercing scream caused her to jump.

"That's it!" she heard Geanie shriek inside the office a moment later.

Cindy paused just outside the door, wondering what on earth was going on.

"I quit!" Geanie screamed.

The door flew open and her roommate ran past her crying.

7

So much for normal, Cindy thought, as she turned
to see where Geanie was running to. Her friend was
making a beeline for the parking lot and after only a
moment's hesitation Cindy chased after her.

"Geanie, wait!" she called.

The other woman didn't slow up, though. By the
time Cindy made it to the parking lot, Geanie was already
speeding away. She stood for a moment watching her car
as it left the parking lot. Then she glanced around
nervously, checking to see if the black car from earlier
had returned.

It wasn't there which made her feel a little bit
better as she stood debating what to do. Should she go
after Geanie? She didn't even know if she was heading
home or somewhere else, though.

She pulled her phone out of her purse and dialed
Geanie's phone. After several rings it went to voicemail.

"It's Cindy. Call me and tell me where you are. I
want to help." She hung up feeling frustrated and useless.

She turned on her heel and headed back to the
office. Maybe she could at least find out what had
happened. As she neared the office door she heard raised
voices. Before she could go inside Dave quickly walked
up to her and shook his head.

"Come with me to the Youth Room," he said.

Cindy hesitated for only a moment before
following him. She didn't know who was arguing in the
office, but she did know that she didn't want to be a part
of it. Once inside the Youth Room Dave closed the door
and led her through the large room which had scattered

couches and massive pillows and beanbag chairs all over the floor.

In the very back of the room was his office and she took a seat on the couch as he collapsed into the chair behind his desk. It was only then that she realized that his hands were shaking.

"Dave, what happened?" she asked, leaning forward.

"Geanie quit."

"I heard her yell that, but I don't know why. I didn't get a chance to talk to her."

He grabbed a bottle of antacids off his desk and popped a couple in his mouth. After he had finished chewing he looked at her. "Royus."

She stared, waiting for more of an explanation.

"They've been going at it for the last hour or so."

"Was this about the Christmas program still?"

"Yes. Neither side is giving an inch. They've both dug trenches and are settling in."

"No compromise in sight?"

"None," he confirmed. "And then, then they decided to actually fight about how they were going to handle advertising this year."

"Oh no!" Cindy said, her hand flying to her mouth. "I was kidding when I said they were going to take it out on her. She's usually the only bulletproof person on staff."

"Well, apparently she showed up to work today without her magic, bullet stopping vest. She offered a solution that would meet both of their needs and instead of thanking her they both lit into her, accusing her of playing favorites."

"What happened after she said she quit?"

"Roy said she'd always been a flake and Gus said that in a couple of months she'd be marrying a rich guy who could take care of her so there was no need to worry about her."

"You're kidding me," Cindy whispered.

"I wish I was."

"This is ridiculous. Their feud is tearing us apart."

"I know."

"First it's going to decimate the staff and next the church."

"I know."

"We have to find a way to stop them."

"I couldn't agree more," Dave said fervently. "I just don't know what that is at this point."

A text came in on Cindy's phone. She grabbed it out of her purse and looked at the screen. It was a message from Geanie. *I'm home*, it read.

Cindy felt a little bit of relief. Geanie had been in no condition to be driving or wandering around by herself. At least she was somewhere safe which gave her a couple of minutes to think about what her next move should be.

Somewhere not that far off a door slammed hard enough that it shook the building.

"I guess one of them has left," Dave noted.

Cindy stood. "I'm taking the rest of the day off. I need to go be with Geanie."

"Okay, but what about the office?"

Cindy grabbed a piece of paper and a black marker off Dave's desk and wrote *Closed for the rest of the day* on it. Next she grabbed a couple of pieces of tape and headed out of Dave's office.

He stood and followed her through the Youth Room. "I agree it's the right thing to do, but Roy will be upset."

Cindy clenched her jaw. "Then he and Gus both just have to learn to live with the consequences of their actions."

She left the room and moments later she was taping the sign on the front of the office door. She walked in, saw that there was no one inside and turned off the coffee pot and the lights. Then she headed back out, locking the door behind her.

She marched out to the parking lot and got in her car. She stared at the entrance to the church for a moment, debating about locking the gates, but decided whoever was there last could handle that matter.

She knew she should tell Roy that she was leaving, but this was her own private act of rebellion. Besides, she reasoned, seeing him while they were both this upset would be a dangerous thing. Who knew what she might actually say to him.

He would figure it out for himself soon enough. In the meantime, she had a friend to take care of.

Minutes later she was walking in the door of her house. Geanie was already in pajamas sitting on the couch in the living room with an entire tub of cookie dough ice cream.

Cindy kicked off her shoes, dropped her purse on the table and went to sit beside her. Wordlessly Geanie handed her an extra spoon.

Ten minutes later there was a knock on the door. Cindy got up to answer it. Joseph was standing there wearing golfing clothes. He came in and made a beeline for Geanie. He sat down on her far side and she handed him a third spoon.

She was prepared, Cindy couldn't help but think as she sat back down and reclaimed her spoon.

They made it to the bottom of the tub of ice cream before any of the three of them said a word. Geanie took the last bite, set the empty carton down on the coffee table, and leaned back against the couch.

"This sucks," she said.

It was like a spell had been broken. Both Cindy and Joseph started asking questions at the same time.

Geanie cleared her throat. "There's nothing either of you can do."

"Dave told me what happened," Cindy said.

Geanie nodded, looking miserable. "What happened after I left?"

Cindy bit her lip. She didn't want to tell her what Dave said Roy and Gus had said upon her departure. "I, uh, closed the office for the rest of the day," she said finally.

Geanie nodded and then glanced at Joseph. "Did I interrupt your game?"

He waved a hand dismissively. "It was just business. It can wait. In fact, if you want, I could reschedule the next few days and we could go to Disneyland Paris or something cool."

"Don't you have a bunch of things you have to do in the next couple of weeks?" Geanie asked.

"Nothing that can't wait."

"What about the dog show?"

Joseph bred and raised champion poodles.

He shook his head. "Clarice could use a break."

"What about the art auction?"

"I have more than enough art already?"

"What about that play we were going to go see?"

"We can see it some other time."

Geanie nodded, but didn't say anything else to him. She turned to look at Cindy. "Why do they have to be like that?" she asked.

Cindy shook her head. "They've been like that since I first got there. I don't know why, I'm just tired of it hurting everyone but them."

Geanie nodded again and turned to stare at the empty carton of ice cream.

"Who wants some mint cookies and cream? There's some in the fridge."

Jeremiah was tired. He had finished the top of the second wall that morning and he was grateful that he was able to ditch the ladder again for a while. Of course, when he got to the bottom of the wall he'd be sitting on the ground again, scooting along as he read. Heinrich certainly hadn't made this easy.

All the worrying he was doing about Cindy wasn't helping either. He was going to call her after work and see how she was. He couldn't spend a lot of time on the phone, but he could at least check in.

His thoughts shifted to what he had found in the master bedroom the night before. A panel from the Amber Room, it had to be. In 2003 a replica of the room had been made and installed at the Tsarskoye Selo State Museum Reserve outside of St. Petersburg. He had seen it once, marveling at the beauty and the intricacy of detail.

Several different groups had been hunting for the real Amber Room after it was lost in 1943. It had last been known to have been at the Königsberg's castle museum in Germany where it had been on display before the museum's director, Alfred Rohde, was told to crate it back up and remove it. It was boxed up and several months later the castle was destroyed by an allied bombing raid. Some believed the Amber Room had been destroyed in that raid but no pieces of wreckage from it had been recovered. Others believed it had already been moved, but theories abounded as to where it could have gone. It was just possible that part of it, or maybe even all of it, had ended up somehow in America. Stranger things had happened and he had been a witness to many of them.

Many different people had worked long and hard to restore items that had been stolen during the war. Most people thought of the art stolen from Jewish people living in Germany and the countries it invaded. However, other countries besides Russia and other people had been subject to looting. Half of the Hesse Jewels belonging to Prussian royalty and stolen by American soldiers had never been recovered.

So many things lost, perhaps forever. It was one of the great atrocities of war that people often didn't think about. The theft and destruction of items of personal and historic value was a travesty.

That was why he had to finish this translating. He had to know what Heinrich had had in his possession and where to find all of it. He only hoped that the information was there.

When he had entered the house that morning it had taken all the strength he had not to tear up the carpets in every room looking for more pieces of the Amber Room. He was sure Mark had already been thinking along the same lines. He'd have to confer with the detective about it a little later.

For now, though, he needed to get through this translation in the hours left to him before the Days of Awe were upon him. Marie was already furious that he wasn't in the office tending to matters in preparation for them.

At least he had made it to the end of the war. Heinrich, who had ultimately joined the military, had managed to slip through the cracks in the final days and had returned to his family's home.

Jeremiah went and got himself a glass of water. His throat was getting tired from the constant talking. At least he didn't have to speak loudly into the recorder. While he drank it he wandered into the dining room. After a moment he realized he was scanning the carpet to see if he could detect any suspicious bumps. He walked slowly over the whole thing but couldn't see or feel anything out of the ordinary.

Frustrated, he returned to the translating. "I became very much of interest in the things that I have seen and the things others have seen that have been done to my parents' brewery. I begin to wonder if there might be something I can take for myself to help make new life somewhere else. One night I took shovel and set out determined to uncover truth if nothing else."

Jeremiah could feel himself starting to get excited. Maybe Heinrich would finally reveal what it was he wanted to know. His throat was raspy and his eyes were tired but he pushed forward.

"What I find that first night not so much. What I find second night equally poor. But third night was everything more than even dreams can be made of. What I find is beyond measure. I know I must keep secret or lose my life. I am good at secrets. Good at finding and good at keeping."

You'd have to be if you managed to smuggle part of the Amber Room out of Germany and into the United States without anyone being the wiser, Jeremiah thought to himself.

He was tempted to skim ahead, but that wouldn't help him finish his work in time. He kept reading. "I know others will come for what I have. I must protect. I must hide. I must move. I think to myself where will no one look for these things. I know the answer to be America. So this presents new problem for solving. I feel myself equal to task for reward is great and failure is to die."

He kept going and after a few more minutes realized that Heinrich was steadfastly refusing to mention what exactly it was that he had found. He ground his teeth in frustration.

Maybe that would come later, though, when he talked about hiding his treasure in America. His stomach growled and he realized that it was past lunchtime. He hadn't brought anything with him and he realized now that was a mistake. He couldn't take the time to leave and go get something. He'd just have to wait until dinner.

He kept going until his voice was nearly ready to give out. Something had to give and if he wasn't careful it was going to be him. He sighed and got some more water. He'd have to get some honey and lemon for his throat.

He grabbed his phone and after only a moment's hesitation he texted Cindy. *Any chance I can get you to bring pizza again tonight?*

A minute later she replied.

Absolutely. Anything else?

Something for tired, sore throat. Honey, lemon, and hot tea would be great.

Will do.

Thx.

I can come early.

What about work? he texted.

Left early. Explain later.

R U OK?

Yes.

See you at 4?

Yes.

He shoved his phone back into his pocket. He could hold out until then, but he needed to rest his voice for a couple of more minutes now.

He found himself once again in the dining room staring at the carpet. It was only a matter of time before he pulled an edge up to see what was underneath. He shook his head. He had nothing else to do while giving his voice a break. He crouched down in the far corner and tugged.

The carpet seemed to be anchored down well. He moved slowly down the wall, feeling every few inches. Then he moved to the next wall. At last he had made his way all around the room. The carpet was tacked down really well. The only way he'd be able to see what was under it was to cut it. His hand slipped to his one pocket where he kept a Swiss army knife. In two seconds he could answer his question for good.

Then it would be a simple matter to test the floors in every other room of the house. If there were more pieces of the Amber Room present he could find out in about two minutes.

He moved his hand away from the knife. He wasn't ready to go that far without the detective's permission. At least, not just yet at any rate. He got up and headed back into the writing room and tried to estimate just how long it was going to take him to finish. He didn't like his odds of completing it.

It was time to get some more help.

It had been good to sit and talk things over with another cop. They had ended up having several cups of coffee while they talked. Mark had sorely missed Paul in that regard as well. It seemed wrong to be working cases alone and it helped to have someone to bounce ideas off of. Liam seemed to be a good guy and a good cop. He could go far in his chosen profession so long as nobody shot him first.

Liam's phone rang and he answered it. He talked for less than a minute and when he hung up he looked disappointed.

"What's wrong?" Mark asked.

"After the trap door was found yesterday I asked a friend of mine to find me any information on the house that he could, when it was built, by who. I wanted to see if maybe there was anything else like that we should be looking for."

Mark raised an eyebrow in surprise. "That was some real initiative," he said. He left out that it was also overstepping. "So, what did they find out?"

"It was built 15 years ago. The contractor and three of his crew died in a car crash just a couple of days before it was finished."

"Tough luck."

Liam laughed. "Maybe it really is part of the Amber Room that was found. Some say there's a curse on it."

"Get something flashy enough or famous enough and everyone's bound to start finding curses connected to it. I wouldn't put too much stock in that," Mark said. He glanced at his watch. "It's time to get back to it," Mark said, standing and getting ready to leave the coffee shop.

"If there's anything I can do to assist you, let me know," Liam said.

"I appreciate it, but do yourself a favor and make sure your days off stay your days off. This job... it's too easy to let it suck you in and consume you. You need to take the time off for your own sanity and that of those around you. You understand?"

"Yes, and thank you for the advice."

Mark's phone rang and he pulled it out of his pocket. "The rabbi's calling," he said.

Liam nodded as Mark answered.

"Hello, tell me you have some good news."

"I'm not calling with news, I'm calling because I need some help here," the rabbi said.

"I'll send the secretary over. I'm sure she'll bring food, extra batteries for the recorder, whatever you need."

"No, I need help translating. You have to find someone else to help me with this."

"Sorry, I've checked, there's no one but you."

Another call was coming in. He'd have to call whoever it was back.

"I have a hard time believing that," Jeremiah said. "There must be someone you can get."

"It's the truth."

It was a lie. Mark hadn't checked. The rabbi was doing a great job and he wanted to make sure they maintained quality control and consistency of translation throughout. Plus he just didn't have time to find someone qualified and meet with them in order to determine whether or not he could work with them.

"So, have you found something interesting for me?" Mark asked.

"Lots interesting, but I'm not sure if any of it is helpful at this point."

"Well, keep going, I know you can do it."

"Thanks," Jeremiah said sarcastically.

"You're welcome," Mark said brightly before hanging up.

He checked his voicemail. A creepy, oily sounding voice began to speak and he felt his lips curling even as he forced himself to listen.

"Detective, I think you'll find your blood results from the wrapping around the painting to be very interesting. Let's just say they belong to an old friend."

He deleted the message and glanced at Liam.

"It's Gordon," he said making a face.

"Who?" Liam asked.

"One of the lab guys, specializes in blood typing, DNA analysis, that sort of thing.

"Gordon...is that his last name or first name?"

"I honestly don't know."

"I don't think I've met him," Liam said.

"Probably not. They don't let him out of his cage that often to interact with people."

Liam looked surprised and almost offended by the remark.

"He's a bit of a ghoul," Mark explained.

"What makes you think so?"

"Well, among other things, he collects celebrity blood samples."

"That's... disturbing," Liam said, making a face.

"I told you."

"Where does he even get his items?"

"I don't ask and thank heavens he doesn't tell."

Mark took a deep breath and called back. When he was alive Paul had always been the one to interface with Gordon.

Gordon answered with a cackling laugh. "Can't wait to hear what I have to say, can you?"

"No, Gordon, I really can't," Mark said, gritting his teeth. *If I could, I would*, he added to himself.

"I finished my analysis and I think you'll find the results very intriguing."

Mark didn't want to be on the phone with him any longer than he had to be.

"Skip to the punch line. Whose blood is it?"

"Mike Haverston, that art dealer who got killed last year."

Mark froze. "You're kidding me."

"No, I'm not," Gordon practically purred into the phone.

Mark ended the call.

"What is it?" Liam asked.

"The first new evidence in the Haverston case since November."

"Which is?"

"It was his blood on the wrapping for the dog painting."

Mark called Jeremiah's cell.

"What is it?" the rabbi asked on picking up.

"You sound terrible."

"I noticed."

"Have you come across any references to a Mike Haverston or to art dealers?"

"No."

"Well, keep looking and tell me if something comes up."

Mark hung up and headed for his car.

"Where are you going?" Liam asked.

"To ask Mike's kids what their dad had to do with an old Nazi."

From the expression on Liam's face he could tell the other officer wanted to go with him. More surprising, Mark actually wanted him to come along. That didn't make it a good idea, though. When he reached the car he turned.

"I meant what I said earlier. Enjoy your days off. We don't get nearly enough of them. And someday if you go for detective and make it you'll find that you would give anything to have those days back."

Liam nodded solemnly, but he could still see the disappointment in his eyes. Mark felt bad, but he was doing right by the other guy. In the end that was what really mattered.

Mark left and his thoughts were quickly consumed by the task at hand. By the time he pulled up outside the Haverston & Sons art gallery he was prepared to ask some tough questions.

There was a sign in the window advertising the upcoming auction. Haverston & Sons had been around for a very long time. The previous owner, Mike, had been one of the titular sons, sole proprietor once his father and older brother passed away. Now his son and two daughters were each joint owners. Mark wasn't at all surprised that all of them were eager to sell everything, get their money, and get out. None of them had struck him as the type who wanted to lower themselves to the status of business owner and pillar of the community.

Of the three of them the son, Trevor, was at least the more reasonable and Mark was glad to find that he was the one who was in and talking with a representative for the auction house that would be handling the whole affair.

Trevor looked surprised to see him, but he managed not to make any sarcastic comment in front of the very attractive blonde lady who was holding a briefcase and clipboard. It was pretty clear from their body language that Trevor had been flirting with her and that she could care less.

Nice to see he didn't get everything he wanted.

"Would you excuse me for just a minute?" he asked the woman who nodded while she continued to study her clipboard.

He gestured for Mark to follow him to the back of the store where the office was. Apparently he had no desire to discuss his father's murder in front of the lady. That was fine with Mark.

They walked into the office but Trevor didn't close the door. He leaned against the desk, arms folded across his chest in classic defensive posturing.

"Are you here because you finally figured out who killed my father?"

"We have a possible new lead," Mark said.

Trevor's eyes actually widened in surprise though the rest of his face remained carefully neutral. "What is it?"

"I'd rather not say at the moment, it's probably nothing, another dead end, but it brought up a few questions I think I forgot to ask originally."

"Go ahead."

"I was going over my notes and I just needed to confirm a few things first. There wasn't anything stolen from the store, correct?"

"That's correct."

"So we have to assume it wasn't an attempted burglary or art heist or anything like that."

"It would stand to reason," Trevor said.

"I believe that most sales happened just from people walking in the store, correct?"

"Correct."

"Now, the paintings that were here when he died are the ones going up for auction, is that right?"

"Yes."

"I got the auction catalogue, by the way, thanks for sending it."

"I didn't. It was probably one of my sisters."

"Well, in that case, thank them for me."

"I know very little about art, so you can just sum up for me what kind of works he had here in the store?"

"My father kept a variety on hand. He always said art was for all the people, not just the ones who could afford it. He sold some originals, a few by well-known artists and others by up-and-comers. Most of the art was lithographs and giclées, high-end reproductions, many with personal accents and touch-ups by the artists.

"What was the most expensive piece he had in the store?"

"I was just discussing it with the lady from the auction house. There's an original Coleman valued at about sixty thousand."

"Impressive."

"It would have been more impressive if he had been actively trying to sell it. It was the one piece of art he kept for himself. It hung in this office until last week," Trevor said.

"He must have loved being able to share art with the world through this store."

Trevor shrugged. "He did his duty, selling art, carrying on the family business. But his passion was always in art restoration."

"Restoration?" Mark asked, more sharply than he had intended to.

"Yes."

"As in fixing damaged pieces?"

"Occasionally. Most of the time it amounts to little more than cleaning them to remove years of dirt or smoke."

"How much does something like that cost?"

Trevor shrugged. "It really depends on how much damage and what type have been sustained. Why, Detective, do you have a piece that needs some work done on it?"

"Maybe," Mark said. "My wife inherited a painting from an uncle and he was a heavy smoker."

It was a lie, but he wasn't about to tip his hand.

"I can give you the name of someone if you'd like."

"I'd appreciate that," Mark said, forcing himself to smile. "You don't do that kind of work?"

"No," Trevor said, rolling his eyes. "You have to truly love art to want to do that."

"And you don't?"

"I appreciate art for what it represents, and that's money."

"I'm surprised, I figured all you Yale types were into that."

"Harvard."

"Excuse me," Mark said.

"I went to Harvard Business School."

"Oh."

Mark had thought that was the case but was pleased to have it confirmed for him without raising Trevor's suspicions.

"Was your father working on any restoration projects for clients when he was killed?"

"No, there was nothing in his studio," Trevor said, blinking rapidly.

He's lying, Mark realized.

"I respect his creed that art should be for all the people. I get that's where the bulk of his business came from, but did he have any really high-end clients? Either for private sales or restoration projects?"

"Not since my father took over the store. I believe my grandfather had a more exclusive clientele and dealt in pieces that were a bit more pricey, but my father changed the business model once it was his sole responsibility."

Just by listening to the emphasis he placed on his words Mark had the distinct impression that Trevor preferred his grandfather's approach. Maybe in the Haverston family snobbery skipped every other generation.

"And now you're shutting it down."

"I don't care to own a business like this," Trevor said. "Too much work, not enough reward."

"Your sisters feel the same way?"

"Of course. Now, what does all this have to do with the new lead you're following?"

"Probably nothing," Mark said.

"Well, if there's nothing else, I really am very busy getting ready for the sale," Trevor said.

"Of course. If I can just get the name of that art restorer from you."

Trevor moved around the desk, opened one of the drawers, and a minute later handed him a card with the information. "Good luck with your wife's painting, Detective."

"Thanks. You know, cleaning it is probably going to cost more than the thing's even worth. It's a picture of a bunch of dogs playing poker."

He swore he saw the nerve under Trevor's eye twitch.

"I'm sure if it has sentimental value to your wife it will be well worth the cost."

"Yeah, thanks."

Mark left, nodding to the lady from the auction house as he passed by her on his way out of the store. She had her cell phone out, looking at it, and she acknowledged his head nod with a tight-lipped smile.

Mark went over the conversation with Trevor in his head. There was something truly fishy, but he needed to put a few more pieces of the puzzle together before he could haul Trevor down to the precinct and accuse him of anything.

He had purposely decided not to mention Heinrich so as to avoid tipping his hand too much. He wondered, though, what would have happened if he had.

Jeremiah was never going to finish the translation work before Rosh Hashanah. He could probably finish reading it to himself by then, but not speaking it into the recorder. He was losing his voice and he couldn't afford to have it gone completely. Not at this time of the year.

He called Mark again.

"Find something?" the detective asked.

"No, you?" Jeremiah whispered.

"Maybe. You sound worse."

"Can you get a video recorder?"

"I'm sure I can scrounge one up for you. I can have it over there in about an hour or so, maybe less."

"Thanks."

Jeremiah hung up, not wanting to waste more words than he had to. He had to sit and rest his voice for a few more minutes before he could resume. He grabbed a glass of water and had a seat in the writing room, in the corner farthest from where the body had been. As he sipped the water he glanced around the room and let his mind wonder.

Rosh Hashanah was the Jewish New Year and was a two-day event. It was the beginning of the ten-day period referred to as Yamim Noraim, the Days of Awe, which some also called the Days of Repentance. The ten days ended with Yom Kippur, the Day of Atonement. The entire time was one of reflection, a time to set goals for the new year and to seek the forgiveness of G-d and others.

He had planned to spend the last few days in quiet contemplation of his own life and preparation for the liturgy he'd be giving. Much of Rosh Hashanah was actually spent in the synagogue.

This year, as always, he had a lot of repenting to do. What he had yet to figure out was what he planned on doing differently in the coming year. He could always pledge not to kill anyone, but with Cindy's penchant for finding trouble that might be an unrealistic pledge. He didn't want to make a vow to G-d knowing there was a real likelihood that he'd have to break it.

Maybe one of the things he needed to rethink was his relationship with Cindy. He had managed to live a low key life for the last few years until she entered into it.

She had definitely shaken things up and changed the balance and order of his life. Because of her he'd done things that he'd never thought he'd have to do again. Then he had nearly kissed her.

Yes, his relationship with her, whatever it actually was, should definitely be the top thing on his list to discuss with G-d. He had brought Cindy into Jeremiah's life and the rabbi did not believe in coincidences. That meant that in all the craziness, all the sheer insanity of the past year-and-a-half there had been a plan, a higher purpose. He just wished he understood what that was.

He thought again of the moment when he'd almost kissed Cindy. It had been so spontaneous, so honest, and it had seemed the most natural thing until he realized what it was he was about to do. It would have changed everything between them and that was something he couldn't allow to happen.

He had always known that caring for a woman, getting close to her in a romantic way would be a complicated thing because he'd have to share with her his past. The burden of it would drive most away.

Lately though he'd had moments where he almost wished he could tell Cindy the truth. Then he would imagine the way she would look at him afterward, the horror in her eyes, the fear in every line of her body, and he knew he couldn't do that. Not to either of them.

He couldn't have a deeper relationship without telling her and there would be no hope of having a deeper relationship once she knew. He was stuck exactly where he was. Somehow that must be in G-d's plan, too. He just hoped that one day soon he knew what that plan was.

Even a tiny glimmer of it would make life so much better.

He finished his water and got back to work. He did a couple of quick tests with the recorder to see just how softly he could whisper before it became an issue. Armed with that knowledge he continued his work.

His stomach rumbled and he hoped that Cindy showed up soon with food. He also hoped Mark showed up soon with the video recorder. In the back of his mind playing over and over he was also wondering just how long he was going to be able to hold out before he pulled up all the carpets in the house looking for more treasure.

It was beyond frustrating that Heinrich still hadn't said what it was that he had found and his optimism that sooner or later the man would write about it was dwindling. His curiosity about the Hebrew writing, though, was only growing. Someone like the ex-Nazi was the last person he'd expect to have made the effort to learn Hebrew. Wherever he had learned it, he had studied hard and done well. He had an impressive vocabulary for someone who hadn't been raised with it. Maybe he would at least find out what had driven the man to learn it.

After the ice cream headaches subsided, Joseph volunteered to take both Cindy and Geanie out to dinner. Cindy declined so that she could take pizza to Jeremiah like she'd promised, but wished them a happy evening. Geanie was at least looking a little bit better than she had been earlier and with Joseph she was in good hands.

She grabbed some packets of tea, a mug, kettle, lemon and honey. She had nearly forgotten that Jeremiah had asked her to bring those things. She just hoped that his throat was doing okay.

She wished she could spend some time online looking up information about the Amber Room, but she remembered that Jeremiah had wanted her to come over early if she could. Her research would just have to wait. But now that some of the shock of the night before and Geanie's pronouncement was wearing off she found herself growing increasingly curious. Was it really possible that the old man had stolen cultural treasures in his home?

From what Jeremiah had been reading Heinrich had clearly fought in the war. She'd heard somewhere that a lot of the art, jewelry, and even silverware that the Nazis had stolen had never been found. Was it possible some of it had made it to America?

It made a certain sort of sense after all. Everyone was busy tracking stuff down in Germany and neighboring countries. Who would even think to look for most of those things in America?

Her curiosity was reasserting itself and she started to get excited about the thought of continuing to search the house for anything else Heinrich could have hidden in it. Of course, at this point, the police had probably already ripped up the rest of the carpet in the house looking for more treasures and trapdoors.

She thought about the painting of the dogs. Why go to all the trouble to hide it? Hiding the Amber Room made perfect sense, but not the painting. You could get a good copy of that for twenty bucks or less at a print shop.

If it had been the bloodstains that were the issue why hadn't he just gotten rid of the paper? He could have thrown it away, burned it, even dissolved it. Unless he didn't have time to do any of those things. Still, she had the impression that the painting had been in its hiding place for a little while, although maybe she was wrong about that.

She swung by and grabbed a large pizza and some more sodas from Round Table and headed on to the house. She was eager to hear what else Jeremiah might have found out while translating.

She pulled up outside, got out of her car and froze. There, halfway down the block, was a black car with dark windows that looked just like the one she had seen in the church parking lot.

Her heart began to beat faster as she continued to stare. For one insane moment she wondered what would happen if she walked up and knocked on the window. She even took a step forward before she stopped herself.

Don't be an idiot, she told herself. It was probably a coincidence and if it wasn't then knocking on the window was the worst thing she could possibly do. The way it was parked behind another car she couldn't read the license plate number and she dare not risk getting close enough to see it.

She got her pizza and drinks out of the car, locked it and headed for the front door still keeping one eye on the black car. She made it inside and Jeremiah greeted her at the door, this time calmly and with a smile which relieved her to no end.

"Everything okay?" he asked, his smile quickly turning to a frown as he studied her face.

"I guess. There's a black car out there with tinted windows. It looks a lot like one I saw in the church parking lot that seemed out of place to me."

He moved past her and outside. She debated about following him, but decided to carry the food into the kitchen. After all, it was probably nothing. As soon as she set things down she headed to the master bedroom, wanting to see what it looked like with the floor torn out.

The sound of a gunshot brought her up short. She turned and took two quick steps toward the front door before it flew open. Jeremiah was standing there, his hand pressed over his upper arm. Blood was dripping between his fingers.

"Call the police!" he gasped.

9

Cindy's scream reverberated through the house as Jeremiah sunk slowly to a seat on the stairs. The sound pained him far more than his arm. He listened as she frantically called Mark and then was unable to stop her from calling 911. As soon as she had hung up with them he got her attention.

"Can you get me a clean towel from the bathroom?"

She ran to get it and was back moments later. Her pupils were dilated and she was breathing in short, shallow gasps. He was afraid that she was going to pass out before he did. He had been going to enlist her help to get the bleeding stopped but immediately thought better of it.

He took the towel from her and pressed it to his arm, applying as much pressure as he could in an effort to stop the bleeding.

"I need you to try to slow your breathing down," he said, making his voice as low and soothing as he could. "I'm going to be okay, the wound isn't bad, I just need to get the bleeding to stop and everything will be fine."

She still had the deer in the headlights look, but at least she was listening to him. He also noticed she was attempting to focus on her breathing.

"Good, that's it," he said.

The shock was wearing off and the pain was crashing in. No matter how many times he was shot he would never get used to it. Sweat was beginning to form on his brow and he knew he had to look incredibly pale, but he struggled not to let her see how much pain he was in. It would do neither of them any good.

His head was swimming a little bit which was not good.

"You're doing good," he reinforced.

"What happened?" she asked, voice barely more than a whisper.

"You were right about the car. There was definitely something suspicious about it. When I got close someone shot me out the passenger window and then the driver took off."

He had been an idiot. He had assumed given everything that she was going through that Cindy was just being paranoid so he had taken no precautions when approaching the car. He hadn't even gotten very close when the occupants reacted.

If he hadn't seen the barrel of the good a split second before it was fired he'd be dead. She didn't need to know that, though.

And no matter what condition she was in he would never again take anything she said lightly. She had incredible instincts about these things and he had just learned the hard way that it was to his detriment to ignore them.

"I'm so sorry!"

"It's not your fault. You weren't the one who shot me. In fact, you warned me that there was something strange about that car. At least now we know that we're being watched, that we need to take precautions. I think part of our problem has been that since neither of us discovered a body we've felt like we were only tangential to this investigation, but I think we just got pulled right into the middle of it."

"I knew something terrible was going to happen," she said, her voice shaking.

"Cindy, we can't focus on that right now," he said. "We just have to stay calm until Mark and the paramedics arrive."

Which couldn't happen too soon as far as he was concerned. The pain was growing and although the bleeding was slowing it wasn't fast enough. There were a few tricks he knew to rectify the latter problem, but he didn't have the tools for most and he was more than a little worried about freaking Cindy out. Seeing him cauterize his own wound was probably more than she could handle at the moment. And the questions she was likely to ask afterward were far more than he could handle ever.

"Tell you what, why don't you humor me and rip up a piece of that carpet in the dining room?" he asked.

She blinked at him. "You want me to rip up the carpet?"

He nodded. "How else are we going to find out if there's treasure under it? Besides, we've got to do something while we wait."

She crouched down and began grabbing at the carpet and tugging on it. "It's tacked down tight," she said.

"Probably a sign that there's nothing to find, but why take the chance?" he asked. "There's a Swiss army knife in my right pocket if you want to get it."

She licked her lips nervously as she stood and walked over to him. Her eyes strayed to his bloody arm.

"Hey, look at me, look me in the eyes," he ordered, putting authority in his voice and raising it slightly even though it hurt to do so because of how hoarse he'd become.

She did as told and he forced himself to smile like he didn't have a care in the world.

"See, everything's good. Now just reach into my pocket and grab the knife."

She looked down and he twisted as far as he could onto his left hip to make it easier for her to reach. She hesitated for the longest moment and then she finally reached into his pocket. He noticed that she started blushing as she did so and it took all his willpower not to comment on it.

She pulled the knife free and stepped back quickly, her cheeks still stained with red.

"You ever use one of those things?" he asked.

She nodded and a moment later had flipped open one of the blades. Then she got down on the ground and attacked the carpet with such ferocity that it was breathtaking. She stabbed and cut and ripped as if her life depended on it.

Moments later she pulled up a hunk of the carpet. Her shoulders dropped slightly. "There's nothing underneath it," she said, disappointment thick in her voice.

"Okay, maybe not under that one, but there's lots more rooms," he said. "Save the writing room for last since they might still be needing to preserve the crime scene."

She nodded and turned toward the stairs. Jeremiah moved his feet slightly so that she could get at the carpet on the first stair. When she pulled it up he saw only wood, no amber reflecting the light as he had secretly hoped to see.

"Why don't you check the rooms upstairs?" he suggested.

He was getting woozier, but keeping her calm and occupied was top priority.

She hesitated. "I don't want to leave you alone," she said after a minute.

"You won't. You'll be right up there and I promise I'm not going anywhere. I'll wait right here."

He smiled again, but from the way she recoiled slightly he realized he wasn't doing a good job of looking calm anymore. She hesitated, but finally walked up the steps, scooting around him, her legs brushing against his good shoulder as she made her way upstairs.

Moments later he heard her attacking the carpet on the landing. There was a ripping sound and then she called down, "Nothing so far."

"Keep looking!"

Finally in the distance he could hear sirens. He heaved a sigh of relief. Time seemed to dilate and stand still after that so it seemed like he had been hearing the sirens for at least an hour. When Cindy came back downstairs it seemed like she was taking a step a minute and each footfall felt like it would shake apart the entire staircase.

"There was nothing," she said, her voice sounding like it was slow and distorted.

He nodded and it felt as though the weight of his own head would send him tumbling forward.

The door opened and Mark entered with paramedics close behind him.

"It's about time," Jeremiah said, his own tongue feeling thick as he slurred the words.

One paramedic grabbed the blood soaked towel and Jeremiah relinquished his hold and felt himself falling backward onto the stairs. He heard Cindy scream from somewhere far off while he debated whether or not to let himself pass out. The pain was great and he was in good hands now so he could, but it would only frighten Cindy more.

With a pained grunt he decided that he had to stay conscious for her sake. Things became clearer. Time seemed to resume to its normal speed and he could clearly hear Cindy telling Mark everything she knew about what had happened.

He could feel hands on him and ripping sounds as the paramedics cut his shirt off of him. There was a moment of silence and then someone whistled low.

"I've never seen so many scars and bullet holes on one person," one of the paramedics was saying. "Who is this guy?"

"He's a rabbi," Mark said, but he heard the uncertainty in the detective's voice.

A better question would be what *hadn't* happened to him.

"Will he be okay?" Cindy asked.

"He'll be just fine," one of the paramedics reassured her. "He'll just have another scar to add to his collection."

"What's one more?" Jeremiah said, attempting to joke.

He opened his eyes and saw them all staring at him. There'd be no escaping rigorous questioning from both Mark and Cindy over what they were seeing. He wasn't looking forward to it in the least.

"You're conscious?" Mark asked.

"Yeah. I am. And I'd really like something for the pain now."

Mark swore under his breath as one of the paramedics reached for a syringe. Jeremiah couldn't hear him, but he could read his lips and he was very glad that Cindy likely couldn't hear him either.

"Miss, can I ask you to step into the other room?" the paramedic with the dark hair asked.

"Careful, that's my wife you're talking to," Jeremiah tried to joke. It was an old joke between Cindy, Mark and him. He'd once had to claim to be her husband in order to see her in the hospital and help protect her from the killer who was after her.

Neither Cindy nor Mark laughed, though, as he had expected them, too. Both looked frightened. He glanced down. There was quite a lot of blood.

"Detective, there's something else you should know."

"What is it, Jeremiah?" Mark asked intently, although his eyes kept straying to the scars on Jeremiah's chest.

"The car...it had diplomatic plates."

This time the detective didn't bother to keep his swearing to himself.

Mark felt as though everything in his world had just been turned upside down. A strange case had just gotten far stranger than he could have ever guessed. Diplomatic plates? Why was someone from another government taking shots at the rabbi? What was someone like that even doing in Pine Springs? There were consulates in Los Angeles but that was an hour away at best.

Then there was the fact that he couldn't take his eyes off Jeremiah. The rabbi's chest looked like it had gotten into a fight with a meat grinder and lost. He wondered how many of the scars were from the terrible ordeal in March at the camp. That whole thing had cost Paul his life.

Mark knew that Jeremiah and all the kids had been hospitalized for a few days afterward, but because of what he had been facing he'd never had a chance to visit. As he thought about it he realized he'd never even really heard what the extent of Jeremiah's injuries were from that. Guilt flashed through him. He'd been so busy dealing with his own emotional baggage related to the Green Pastures tragedy that he'd never even stopped to truly consider everything Jeremiah must have gone through.

Then, all those months they'd spent together with Jeremiah counseling him so he could get back on the force. The things he'd said, the anger, the frustration, and again he'd never thought to check in with the rabbi and see how he was handling everything that had happened to him.

He honestly couldn't remember a time in his life where he'd felt so small, weak, selfish. He glanced at

Cindy and saw the tears in her eyes. She couldn't take her eyes off the scars either. Mark shook his head slowly. He and Cindy were the ones with the majority of the emotional baggage which made no sense in the larger scheme of things.

Impulsively he reached out and grabbed Jeremiah's right hand. It was sticky, covered in the man's own blood. None of this would have happened if he hadn't gotten him involved. There was no one else to blame this time but himself. He might as well have shot the rabbi himself. Jeremiah looked at him and Mark felt tears stinging his own eyes.

"I swear to you I will make this right," he said.

Jeremiah nodded slowly, but Mark could tell he didn't fully grasp his meaning. That was alright. He'd apologize to him later when things were calm and there was no morphine dulling his senses.

He pulled away and put his arm around Cindy's shoulders. He rubbed her back, belatedly realizing that he was rubbing Jeremiah's blood into her shirt. What a mess the three of them were in. Blood bound them together.

First it had been the blood of a dead man in a church, but that had been just the beginning. Eventually it had been the blood of his partner, Paul, who had given his life trying to save Jeremiah's and the blood of a murderer that Mark had been covered in as he tortured him striving for the same goal. And still the blood kept flowing, coating the three of them. It bound them together. One day, though, would it tear them apart?

He shook his head, trying to rid it of the dark thoughts that were swirling through it, threatening to consume him.

Then the paramedics were putting Jeremiah on a gurney and wheeling him toward the ambulance that was waiting outside. They told him the name of the hospital they were heading to. Mark knew it well.

"We'll follow," he told the driver.

Then he and Cindy watched as the ambulance drove away. Once it was out of sight it was as though some sort of spell was broken. Cindy let out a half sob and leaned back against a wall, bracing her hands on her knees.

Mark glanced down and noticed for the first time a hunk of carpet missing from the dining room floor. "What happened?" he asked, gesturing to it.

She seemed to come awake at that, eyes that had seemed lifeless moments before quickening with thought. "Jeremiah had me cut up sections of the carpet in most of the rooms checking to see if there was anything underneath. We didn't find anything. The only room I didn't touch yet was the writing room. I think he was having me do it to distract me."

"Probably, but I can guarantee he's probably been as curious as me and as anxious to rip up the rest of these carpets. It was all I could do not to rip them up last night," Mark admitted.

"Do you really think he's going to be okay?"

"Yes. He's a fighter, that one," he said around the sudden lump in his throat.

"Why does bad stuff keep happening to us?" she asked.

"I'd give just about anything to have the answer to that myself," he admitted. "I'm going to get a couple of officers out here to check the place out and talk to the neighbors, see if anyone saw anything. Then I'll drive you to the hospital."

Cindy looked like she was about to say something and then stopped.

"What is it?"

"No, it sounds terrible."

"I can practically guarantee you that I've heard worse."

"I don't want to go to the hospital. I just want to go home."

"I can take you there, too," he said.

She shook her head. "No, it's okay. I can drive myself."

She rubbed her eyes. "I'll change clothes and then I'll head over to the hospital."

"I know the rabbi would understand if you waited until the morning to see him."

She pushed off from the wall and he winced as he saw the bloody patch she'd left on it.

"He'd understand, but I wouldn't. Does that make sense?"

Mark nodded. "Believe it or not it does."

"I'll see you later," she said, starting for the door.

"Wait," he said. He went into the bathroom and grabbed a towel and came back with it. He handed it to her. "For your backrest. I touched him and then I rubbed your back and I'm afraid I ruined your blouse."

She took the towel, glanced at the wall where she'd been leaning, and then nodded solemnly. "It's okay. I never really liked this shirt anyway."

As soon as she was out the door Mark called in for some officers to help canvass the area. Maybe someone had seen something. It was a long shot, but it was all they had.

He started to head back to the writing room and paused as he passed the kitchen. There was a pizza and soda on the counter. They were untouched. He grabbed himself a slice and made a mental note to pay Cindy back later. Then he called his wife and let her know that it was going to be another long night.

After that was done he ate a couple of more slices of pizza and washed it down with the soda. A couple of officers arrived and he was actually disappointed one of them wasn't Liam until he remembered that he had lectured him about making sure to take his days off seriously. It was hard to believe that had been just a few hours before.

He rubbed his head. He really needed to talk things over with someone and Jeremiah and Cindy were both out of the question at the moment. He sighed, called the precinct, and got Liam's cell number.

"Hello?" Liam answered.

"It's Mark."

"Detective, what can I do for you?" the other officer said, clearly surprised.

"You can forget the speeches I gave you earlier today and you can get your butt down to Heinrich's house. The case just took a turn for the even weirder and two heads are better than one."

"I'll be there in half an hour, let me just stop and grab some fast food."

"No need. I got pizza here."

"Then I'll be there in fifteen."

"Great."

Mark hung up. He felt bad, involving the other officer more than he should be. At least he was a fellow cop, though. He knew the risks inherent in their line of work. This way if he got someone else shot at tonight it wouldn't be a civilian.

"Baggage," he sighed. "I've got lots and lots of baggage."

While he waited for everyone to arrive he decided he might as well finish the job that Cindy had started. He headed into the writing room and tested the edges of the carpet until he found a section that was loose. When he pulled it up, though, there was nothing special underneath.

It was worth a try, he thought as he dropped the carpet back into place.

He fished in his pocket for his phone, figuring he'd call Cindy and let her know there hadn't been anything. That way she and Jeremiah could at least have their curiosity slaked on that one.

His phone wasn't in his pocket where he normally kept it. He checked his other one and pulled out the piece of paper with the art restorer's phone number on it. He stared at it for a moment before heading into the kitchen where he found his phone where he'd apparently left it next to the pizza box.

Pull yourself together, he ordered.

He called Cindy and left a message when it went to voicemail. Then he went ahead and dialed the number on the card, knowing it was unlikely he would reach anyone this late.

He was surprised when a woman answered the phone. "Hello, this is Melissa."

"Melissa, hi, my name is Detective Mark Walters. I'm with the Pine Springs Police Department."

"Oh," she said, clearly startled. He got it. It wasn't every day that most people had police calling them up out of the blue. "Your name was given to me as someone who does restoration work on art."

"Oh, yes, I do that," she said, warming slightly.

"I'm sorry to call so late. I frankly expected the shop to be closed."

"I work out of my house," she said. "And it's okay. How can I help you?"

"I have a piece of artwork I'd like you to look at for me and give me an assessment."

"Of course. When would you like to come by?"

"At your earliest convenience."

"I can take a look tonight if it's important."

"It is and I would very much appreciate it if you could," he said. "Would an hour from now be alright?"

"Certainly. Do you have my address?"

"No."

"It's 23 Sycamore Terrace. Come around to the side door."

"Thanks. I'll see you then."

He hung up just as the uniformed officers were arriving. He briefed them and told them what he wanted them to ask the area residents. By the time they were getting to it Liam showed up.

He walked in the door, saw all the blood, and stopped. "That's new," he said.

"Yes, unfortunately, it is."

"What happened?"

"I'll fill you in on the way."

"Okay, where are we going?"

"To get the dog picture out of evidence and take it to a lady who restores paintings. I've got a few questions for her."

They climbed into Mark's car and as they drove Mark told Liam about his meeting with Trevor earlier and about Jeremiah being shot. When he got to the part about the car apparently having diplomatic plates Liam whistled low.

"Tell me about it," Mark said. "This day just keeps getting weirder and weirder."

"I'd heard around the precinct that you're always the one who gets the exciting cases."

"Exciting?" Mark snorted. "Try bizarre, terrifying, life altering. I don't know how I got so unlucky, but that's how it seems to play out."

"Is it every case of yours or just the ones that Cindy and Jeremiah get involved with?" Liam asked.

"It's an excellent question and I don't even know how to answer that, especially since a case from a year ago that they had no involvement with whatsoever is now turning out to be part of a case that they are involved with. Maybe the three of us are just cursed," he muttered at the end, thinking of the blood bond he'd imagined earlier.

They retrieved the painting from the station and then headed on to Melissa's studio. A few minutes later they were pulling up outside a large two-story house.

"We're early," Mark said, glancing at the clock on the dash. "She said to go to the side entrance."

They got out of the car and began walking around the house. They finally spotted the side door. It was hard to see. The light above it was dark and there wasn't much light from the street making it back that far.

"Does it strike you as odd that the porch light wasn't on nor this one?" Mark asked.

"You said we're early."

"Still."

Something felt wrong enough that Mark pulled his gun scarcely realizing that he'd done so.

"I didn't bring a weapon," Liam admitted.

"Then stay behind me," Mark ordered, moving in front of him.

They reached the side door. It was closed. There was a doorbell off to the side and Mark rang it then stepped back.

Silence.

"I don't like this," he said.

He tried the door and the knob turned easily.

He pushed it open, staying to the side, and waited. Still nothing.

"Police, is anyone home?" he called.

Ducking down he reached inside and felt for a light switch. His fingers finally brushed a plate with two switches. One was probably for the outside light and one for the inside. He flipped them both and light flooded down on them and illuminated the room inside.

The place had been ransacked. Easels were flipped over, paintings had been slashed, papers had been flung about, and there was brightly colored smears of paint all over the floor.

Keeping his gun trained in front of him Mark stepped into the room, sweeping it with his eyes. The place was a wreck. Whoever had tossed it had been moving fast and not picky about what he destroyed in the process.

"There in the doorway to the left," Liam said.

Mark swung his gun to face that direction.

There, laying face down on the ground, was a woman.

10

Cindy felt like she was moving through a dream as she drove toward the hospital. She had made it home where she had discovered just how much blood was on the back of her shirt. She had started to rinse it in the sink with cold water, but had swiftly changed her mind and thrown it out. She had an intense feeling that she'd never be able to wear it again without reliving, or at least remembering, the events of the evening. She would really rather put that as far behind her as possible. She changed clothes, wolfed down a granola bar she found in the cupboard, and headed out.

Now as she parked outside the hospital she felt somewhat nauseated. She didn't like hospitals and the last several months had only increased her discomfort around them. She owed it to Jeremiah, though, to go inside no matter how much she didn't want to.

She marveled at the fact that she really had reached a point where she just wanted to go to bed, pull the covers over her head, and hide from the rest of the world. As tempting as that sounded, though, it wouldn't do anyone any good, probably least of all her.

She said a quick prayer for her strength as she exited the car then forced herself to march through the front doors as if she didn't mind hospitals in the least. Once inside she went up to the information desk.

"I'm here to see Jeremiah Silverman. He would have been brought into the emergency room about half an hour ago with a gunshot wound to the arm." She marveled at how calm and matter-of-fact she sounded.

The nurse must think she was insane for treating it like no big deal.

The woman looked at her with a little bit of suspicion, or perhaps Cindy's own discomfort and paranoia made it seem that way. Before she could say anything, though, another nurse walked by, stopped and turned back to her.

"Mrs. Silverman. Hi, I was one of your nurses when you were in here a while back. I'll take you right to your husband."

Cindy felt herself turn bright red. Jeremiah had been forced to claim that relationship so he'd be allowed to see her and protect her from a serial killer just days after he and she had first met. She had never forgotten, but she had assumed people at the hospital would.

Still, she didn't say anything, but followed meekly behind as the woman took her through twisting hallways. He was probably still in the emergency section of the hospital and she probably should have parked around that side, she realized belatedly. She felt like she was doing everything in slow motion, particularly thinking.

At last they came to the emergency ward where a long room had several semi-private beds that were screened from each other by curtains.

"I found your wife outside looking for you," the nurse said cheerfully as she ducked through one of the curtains.

Cindy sheepishly followed her and had a hard time meeting Jeremiah's eyes. He was smiling, but he was incredibly pale. He was connected up to all sorts of monitors and there was an IV drip hooked up to his right arm.

"Thanks for bringing her by, I was beginning to wonder when she was going to get here," Jeremiah said, sounding weak.

"Sorry it took so long," Cindy said, feeling guilty.

He reached out for her and she moved so she could take his hand. "I understand," he said softly.

"The doctor will be with you in a minute," the nurse said before leaving.

"Are you okay?" he asked, rubbing the back of her hand with his thumb.

"I've been better," she admitted.

"I'm glad you came."

"Well, I couldn't very well leave you alone here, could I?" she asked, forcing herself to smile. She'd never tell him that she'd wanted to do just that by hiding at home.

"I know it can't be easy for you," he said, finally letting go of her hand.

She pulled up a chair. "How are you feeling?"

"Better. Now I just have to convince them to let me go home. I'd appreciate your help with that."

"I think you should stay overnight," she argued.

He shook his head. "Can't. Rosh Hashanah starts tomorrow night and I'm behind as it is."

"But you've been shot."

"I'll live. Clearly."

She bit her lip as she thought about seeing him with his shirt off while the paramedics worked on him. There had been so many scars. Small holes, long jagged ones. She had realized even then that the others in the room were shocked by how many scars he had. Some of them were even bullet scars.

"You've been shot...a lot," she said finally.

He studied her quietly for a moment. "You know I spent my required time in the army in Israel."

"I know, everyone there has to serve. I just thought, I don't know, that you'd be doing more chaplain kind of duties."

He gave her what she could only describe as an intensely sad look. "If only things were that simple," he said, his voice sounding strained.

"You were hurt?"

"Yes. I saw combat. It left its mark."

She could tell he didn't want to talk about it.

It didn't just scar his body, she realized.

She wanted desperately to know more, but she couldn't push. She instinctively felt it was hurting him just to admit that much. Before she could say anything the curtain parted and the doctor strode in, his head buried in Jeremiah's chart.

He finally looked up. "You've had a busy evening," he said.

"Yup. Ready to go home now and get some rest."

"I'm not sure that's such a good idea," the doctor said. "I want to keep you overnight."

"That's not acceptable," Jeremiah said.

She winced at his use of the word which made him sound combative instead of persuasive.

"Please," she piped up. "He'd be so much more comfortable at home. He's afraid of hospitals and I know he won't be able to get any rest here. I can make sure he's comfortable and has everything he needs bef-" she cut herself off before she could say the rest of her sentence. She was about to admit that she would be going home and leaving him alone which would virtually guarantee that the doctor would force him to stay overnight where he could have help and supervision.

"And just who are you?" the doctor asked her.

"She's my wife," Jeremiah said, grabbing her hand again.

"I'm sorry, but I feel you really need medical monitoring."

"She was an army nurse in Afghanistan," Jeremiah said. "I'll be just fine."

She blinked, struggling not to let her face give away Jeremiah's lie. It was important enough for him to go home tonight that he was willing to take it that far. She didn't like it, but she wasn't going to contradict him.

"Where'd you serve?" the doctor asked.

"Kandahar," she said the first name that popped into her mind. Her mom had had a second cousin who was there at the beginning of the war. She forced herself to look at him straight on and not blink.

"So, you know a thing or two about gunshot wounds, then."

"You know she does," Jeremiah said. "If she'd been there when this happened I wouldn't have called for an ambulance."

"Please. Rosh Hashanah begins at sundown tomorrow night. We need to prepare. He's a rabbi and it would be devastating if this impacted the most important holy days of the year," Cindy said. "It would severely impair the free exercise of his religious beliefs and those of a great many others."

Jeremiah was practically crushing her hand. She took that as a sign that she was laying it on too thick. She eased off. "Please, we just want to go home," she said.

She felt tears begin to sting her eyes, and those at least were real.

"Honey, could you give us a moment?" Jeremiah asked.

She nodded, wiped at her eyes, and headed outside.

She could hear the two men talking in low voices, but not what they were saying.

A minute later the doctor came out. The look he gave her was one of pity. "I'll release him into your care. I'll write out detailed instructions for dosages and have the hospital pharmacy deliver the prescriptions here right away. I'll leave my number. If anything goes wrong...for either of you...call me at any time day or night and I'll come over."

"Thank you," Cindy said, wondering what on earth Jeremiah could have told him.

He looked like he was about to touch her but then dropped her hand. "I'll have you out of here in thirty minutes," he said.

Mark dearly hoped that the woman on the floor wasn't the one they were there to meet, but he had a feeling given how she dressed that she was indeed the art restorer and the owner of the house.

Liam rushed forward toward the body of the woman. Mark grabbed him by the collar as he passed and pushed him sideways into the wall.

"What the-"

"First, we make sure it's safe," Mark hissed.

They needed to make certain that whoever had done this wasn't still in the house as well as ascertain whether or not the woman was a threat before approaching the body.

There appeared to be only two exits from the room - the door they had come in through and the doorway into the rest of the house that the body was blocking. The space was large but there were no closets for anyone to be hiding in.

Mark edged forward, weapon trained on the fallen woman, eyes darting between her and what he could see of the house beyond. Lights were on in other parts of the house making him think she had entered the room either because she had heard a noise or in preparation for their meeting and surprised the intruder.

He wasn't about to take any chances that that was what had happened, though. When he was standing close to the body he reached out and nudged the shoulder with his toe.

There was no response. He watched the back carefully, but could see no signs of breathing. He shifted so he could kick the leg, just hard enough that if she was alive and conscious it would definitely elicit a response. Again nothing.

He handed Liam his gun and then bent down swiftly and felt for a pulse at the base of her neck. There was none.

He stood and took his gun back from Liam. He stepped over the woman, crouching down as he moved quickly through the doorway and out into the hallway beyond.

He let his eyes sweep down it. He was about to turn and open the door directly across the hallway when he heard a crash from the front of the house.

He ran in a low crouch, weapon trained in front of him. The family room and dining room when he came to them were empty. He glanced up the stairway to the second floor but saw nothing. He passed through the front entrance area of the house and headed for the kitchen.

He heard a soft thud and he tensed, lifting a hand to let Liam who was following behind know to use caution. Mark slowed and stood just outside the kitchen, back pressed against the wall. Sweat was beading on his forehead. He took a deep breath, counted to three, and charged through the doorway.

As Mark dashed through the doorway into the kitchen he wasn't sure who he'd find inside. His finger was on the trigger of his gun and his mind was hyper alert.

His eyes flicked across the room and at first saw no one. Then he dropped them slightly and saw shattered glass on the ground and a pool of white liquid spreading out from it. There, at the edge of the liquid eagerly lapping it up, was a fluffy orange cat.

He felt himself sag slightly with relief. He'd been afraid that someone was about to get hurt, that the killer would fire on him or that he would accidentally fire on some innocent bystander.

He turned to Liam and whispered. "Let's finish clearing the house and then we'll call it in."

Twenty minutes later Cindy was helping Jeremiah into her car. Once inside she headed for the exit of the parking lot.

"I've never seen them discharge someone so quickly," she said. "What on earth did you say to him?"

"I could tell that he wasn't going to cave even if you were an army nurse, so I told him the truth."

"Which is?"

Jeremiah sighed as he leaned his head back against the seat. "That you're suffering PTSD from having been kidnapped and tortured a couple of months ago. I told him you were already afraid of hospitals and that with everything that was happening, I couldn't predict how you were going to react. I also told him he'd be unsuccessful in trying to get you to leave the hospital and that the best solution for us and for them was to let me go home."

"I see. Did you also tell him we weren't married?"

"Not a chance. As far as those people are concerned we're married and it's better for us if they keep thinking that. It's come in handy too many times."

"Oh. Well, at least I don't have to pretend to be an army nurse from now on. That could have gotten awkward."

"You were a real soldier, in there, though. I appreciated it. I'm going to have to make it up to you somehow."

"Steak dinner when this is done," she said.

"You're on."

"And explain to me what Rosh Hashanah is," she said.

He actually chuckled. "I was wondering when you'd ask."

"I'm asking, so talk."

"It's the Jewish New Year, but instead of a time for wild festivities, it's a time for deep reflection on the past year and the coming year."

"So, like resolutions."

"Yes, but ideally a bit more spiritual. Rosh Hashanah begins the ten-day period known as Yamim Noraim, which means the Days of Awe or some would say the Days of Repentance. They end with Yom Kippur, the Day of Atonement. During Yamim Noraim we believe that G-d has books that he writes our names down in and he decides what will happen to you in the coming year, who will die, who will have a good life or a bad life. He writes in these books on Rosh Hashanah and we have until Yom Kippur when the books are sealed to get him to change his mind and rewrite our life for the coming year. That's why I would say to you L'shanah tovah tikatevi v'taihatemi. It means 'may you be inscribed and sealed for a good year'."

"How do you get God to change what he wrote about you?" she asked.

"Good deeds, prayer, and repentance."

"Yom Kippur is the day you atone for your sins?"

"Only those made against God. Before Yom Kippur if you want to atone for sins against another person you must reconcile with them, and right any wrongs that you can."

"It all sounds complicated," Cindy said.

"It's cleansing," Jeremiah countered. "It's starting each year with a fresh slate. Well, as fresh as you can."

"So, what do you do on Rosh Hashanah itself?"

"It's a two day celebration. The shofar, which is like a trumpet but is made out of a ram's horn, is blown in the synagogue one hundred times on each day as a call to repentance. People eat honey dipped apples as they wish for a sweet year. They also symbolically cast off their sins on the first day by emptying their pockets into a stream or other type of flowing water. Usually the pockets are filled with bread crumbs or something of that nature that stand in for the sins being cast off."

"And it's actually considered a holiday, right?" she asked.

"No work is permitted on Rosh Hashanah."

"Which is why you have to get your preparations done before it starts?"

"Exactly. Much of the two days is actually spent in the synagogue and the liturgy is different."

"So, no working unless you're you."

He looked at her. "Well, being rabbi, reading liturgy, that is your job, your work, so you're still stuck working."

"You want to know what's weird?" he asked.

"What?"

"I never actually thought about it that way until right now."

She smiled. "I've been trying to pay attention. It's like Shabbat in that way, too. You're the only one working. So, really, on those days where you're not permitted to work, but people are supposed to go to the synagogue, they should all go and you should stay home and quietly reflect on God or even do something completely different, like golf or something."

"If I weren't in so much pain and on so much medication, I'd be laughing right now," he admitted.

"Then my job here is done. I might as well pull over the car right here," she joked.

"Don't you dare," he said.

"Don't worry. I promised the doctor I'd take care of you and I will. It sounds like a busy time for you, work wise, though. Do you think you'll be able to handle everything in your condition?"

"The hard part will be the day after Rosh Hashanah."

"Why?"

"That's a fast day, the Fast of Gedaliah."

"You've got to be kidding me."

"Wish I was. Fortunately medical exceptions are made. I'll just have to figure out what those are going to be in my case."

"That's a lot to pack in to a few weeks."

"Oh, that's not all. Five days after Yom Kippur is Sukkot which is a big deal. It lasts for seven days and then there are two holidays on the two days following it."

"Stop! Information overload."

"Not surprising," he said.

"Tell you what, let's get through Yom Kippur and then you can tell me about the others."

"Okay," he said.

She glanced over at him. His arm was heavily bandaged and in a sling. She thought again of that moment where she realized he'd been shot.

If we live that long, she silently amended.

It took a few more minutes, but Mark and Liam finally finished sweeping the entire house. No one else was there. They headed back into the room with the body while Mark called it in. When he was finished he looked at Liam who was just staring at him.

"What is it?" he asked.

"You assumed that she was alive and dangerous. Why?"

"Years ago I participated in a drug bust. We were searching the house and I saw a guy laying face down on the floor next to a pool of blood. I dropped my guard, bent down to check on him, and he rolled over and shot me. Fortunately I was wearing my vest, but he was aiming at my head when one of the other officers came up behind me and killed him. That's when I learned never to approach a fallen body without assuming the person could be armed and dangerous."

"Thanks. I will remember that."

"I hope so." Mark took a deep breath. He pulled his keys out of his pocket and tossed them to Liam. "Grab us some gloves. I keep a box in the trunk."

Liam left and Mark stood gazing around the room, anger burning in him. It looked like whoever had done this had been looking for something. She must have surprised whoever it was and they killed her. The real question was, did they find what they were looking for?

He heard running footsteps outside and he drew his weapon.

"Detective!" Liam said, bursting through the door, eyes wide.

"What?"

"Your car...somebody broke into it and stole the painting."

Jeremiah was exhausted. He was in worse shape than he'd let on to either the doctor or Cindy. He'd lost a lot of blood and that was making him weak. They hadn't completely immobilized his arm which meant that he kept inadvertently moving it releasing waves of pain through him that the painkillers could only dull but not get rid of. It was incredibly taxing to have to actively try to keep still and then deal with the pain when he couldn't.

Just getting from Cindy's car into the house was nearly too much for him. He grit his teeth in frustration. He'd had wounds that were far more serious that were still far easier to work around.

As soon as they got in the door Captain walked up whining. He was clearly tempering his usual boisterous greeting because he could tell something was wrong. The dog was incredibly smart and Jeremiah was deeply grateful for that at the moment.

"I think it's straight to bed for you," Cindy said, as she eased him toward the bedroom.

"Sounds like a good idea."

He was wearing his slacks and the hospital gown since his cut up shirt had needed to be thrown out. Cindy helped him sit down on the side of the bed and then she reached down and started taking off his shoes.

"You don't have to do that," he said.

"You really want to jostle that arm around any more tonight?" she asked.

"No," he admitted.

"Then let me do what I can to help."

He decided not to argue. The medication was making him more and more drowsy and he was struggling not to fall asleep where he was sitting. In the car it had been easier because he'd been able to focus on explaining the holidays to her.

As soon as his shoes were off she moved to his sling which she removed. Then she looked at him with an odd expression.

"What?" he asked.

"Where are your pajamas?"

"I'm too tired to get in them, I'll just sleep like this," he said.

"Are you sure?"

He nodded.

"Okay. What can I get you to eat or drink?"

He shook his head. "There's some crackers in the cupboard. If you could just put some of those, a glass of water, and my pills on the nightstand I'll be fine."

"You're not getting rid of me that easily," she said, crossing her arms over her chest.

"Why not?" he asked, realizing he was slurring his words.

"Because you're going to need medication in the middle of the night and from the looks of you I'm not sure you can handle it on your own."

"I don't need the painkillers if I'm sleeping," he protested.

"I'll tell you what. I'll sleep on the couch and that way I can come in and check on you."

"Really, I'm okay," he said, struggling to keep his eyes open. "Just a little too warm in here." He used his good hand to pull off the hospital gown.

145

"Do you want a T-shirt?" she asked.

"No, I'll sleep like this." It would help keep him from bunching the gown too much around the dressing on his arm as well.

Cindy averted her eyes. "Go to sleep and for once, don't worry about me," she said.

He wanted to protest that he always worried about her, but he felt himself falling backward. His head hit his pillow and he sank into sleep.

Jeremiah looked so peaceful Cindy lingered in the room a minute just watching him sleep. She had known he was more out of it than he was letting on. She found an extra blanket and pillow in the linen closet near the bathroom and dropped them on the couch in the living room.

Next she headed into the kitchen and checked out the refrigerator. Jeremiah might not need anything to eat, but she did. From the way Captain eagerly followed her she was guessing he did, too.

She scratched the dog behind the ears and he wagged his tail. She changed the water in his bowl and then gave him fresh dog food.

"I'll take you out after we eat," she said, yawning.

She found some cheese and roast beef in the refrigerator. She didn't see any bread, so she just wrapped the cheese in the roast beef and ate it that way. She downed it with a glass of water.

She took Captain for a quick walk and then went and sat down on the couch. She heaved a sigh and felt exhaustion really take hold of her. Her body felt so heavy and she wondered briefly if she'd be able to even get up off the couch when it was time to give Jeremiah medication.

She pulled out her phone, preparing to set the alarm to wake herself. She had missed calls from both Geanie and Mark.

She called her roommate first and filled her in on what was going on. Thankfully Geanie didn't make any even remotely romantic suggestions. She did, however, offer to bring a change of clothes by.

"Can you do it in the morning? I'm going to crash soon."

"Are you actually thinking of going into work tomorrow?" Geanie asked skeptically.

"Yeah," Cindy said. "Personally, I'd like to stay home, but I have a feeling I'm going to be driving Jeremiah to the synagogue."

"And at that point you might as well save a sick day and go in?"

"That's kind of what I was thinking."

She was also thinking that she'd at least be nearby if he needed her.

After she hung up with Geanie she called Mark.

"Hello?" he answered, voice tense.

"Everything okay?" she asked.

"Not really. Got another body. An art restorer. And the dog painting was just stolen."

"I'm so sorry," Cindy said, at a loss as to how else to respond.

"Not your fault," he muttered. "What's happening there?"

"We're at Jeremiah's. He talked his way out of the hospital because tomorrow evening Rosh Hashanah starts and he has to-"

"Get ready. Yeah, he's been warning me about that for days. You're going to stay there with him, right?"

"I've already made up the couch."

"Good. Call if something goes wrong. Well, more wrong."

"You, too."

"Not likely," he said. "The two of you need rest more than anything. Whatever else happens at this point it can wait until the morning."

"Okay. Be careful."

He paused as if really hearing what she had said. "I will," he said in a different tone.

"Thank you."

"I'll call tomorrow when I can."

"Alright. Good night."

He grunted and hung up.

Cindy set her phone down on the coffee table and stretched out on the couch. Her muscles began to twitch and vibrate as they slowly relaxed. It was a disturbing feeling, but at least they were capable of relaxing somewhat.

Captain walked over and regarded her with big, concerned eyes.

"I'm fine. Go see your dad," Cindy said.

The dog turned and padded off toward the bedroom.

Mark was just about done. Even the other officers were starting to actually look at him. Finally one of them came up to him. "How long since you got some sleep, Detective?"

He grunted an unintelligible reply and the man backed off. They were probably all worried he was getting ready to go off the deep end again.

There was no sign of forced entry so the lady must have let her killer in. Officers were dusting for prints, but he wasn't optimistic that they were going to find any. She had been stabbed in the throat with a ballpoint pen that had her company information on it. The irony was sad really, but he was beyond feeling at that point.

He was trying to make sense of the destruction in her lab. Had the killer actually been looking for something specific or was this done to make it look like a burglary gone bad?

Liam walked up to him.

"How are you holding up?" Mark asked.

"Good. Is there anything you want me to do?" he asked. "I'm still technically off duty and these guys have got things handled."

"No, you can...wait," Mark said. "Was there still a video camera in my trunk when you checked?"

"Yeah, whoever it was took the painting but left that."

"Makes me think that painting, or something like it, was what the killer was after," Mark said.

"It stands to reason."

"Can you take that camera and go over and slowly videotape the writing on the last two walls in Heinrich's house? It's going to take forever, but the rabbi can't go to the site so we have to bring the site to him."

"I can do that."

"Great. And stop by your house and pick up your gun first. Keep your eyes peeled. I don't want you getting shot, too. In fact, keep the gun on you until this case is resolved, even when you're off duty. Got it?"

"I got it," Liam said.

"Great. Take my car. I'll get one of the other officers to drop me over there to get it back from you later."

Liam nodded and headed out after Mark handed him the keys. Mark was glad he'd remembered about the camera. Hopefully he could cajole Jeremiah into finding time to finish the job.

This whole thing was getting more complicated. He just hoped there was something in the old man's writings that would help him figure this all out. What he wouldn't give for a name, but he doubted he'd be that lucky.

When was he ever?

Persistent, throbbing pain woke Jeremiah up in the middle of the night. He came to wake slowly, groggy and struggling to remember what had happened. He heard a whisper of sound in the room and he tried to sit up.

Intense, stabbing pain knifed through his arm and he hissed sharply.

"Ssh, it's alright," a female voice said.

He recognized it and he struggled for a moment to place it before coming more fully awake and realizing it was Cindy. She was standing above him, bathed in silvery moonlight from the curtains that were partially open across the room. She had a look of concern in her eyes and yet she was smiling at him reassuringly. The moonlight was making her hair shine. She had never looked more beautiful and it took his breath away.

She sat down next to him on the bed, so close her leg was brushing his. His heart began to race and the pain was forgotten in a moment.

"It's time to take your medication," she whispered softly.

That was the farthest thing from his mind.

She reached for the water glass on his nightstand and he grabbed her hand instead. The feel of her skin against his was electric.

She needed to know, though, what she was getting herself into. Without that, there could be nothing else.

He pulled her hand down and placed it on his chest. He moved her fingers around, guiding her to different bullet wounds, knife scars.

"What is it?" she asked him, her voice still a whisper.

"You have to know who I was, who I am. I have to tell you."

It was important and he let her hear the urgency in his voice.

"I know who you are," she said, her smile growing even more radiant.

"No, you don't, not really. I have wronged you by not telling you and I'm sorry. I just never expected...you."

"What do you mean?"

"I was not a nice person before I came here. I did things, things you can never forgive me for."

"You were in the army."

"No, I did not do these things in the army."

He had to tell her even as the nearness of her was filling his senses, making him crazy. He had been so afraid to tell her for so long, but if he did not tell her and he took her in his arms he would be sinning against her and G-d. If she came to him it had to be willingly, of her own choice, with all the knowledge he could give her so that she knew what she was doing.

He moved her hand around to more of the scars, her touch making his skin tingle. "This is from the army," he said, moving her fingers over a jagged knife wound over his ribs, "from hand-to-hand combat training. My training partner was faster than I, more aggressive. He gave this to me. The rest I did not earn in the army."

"I do not understand."

He let go of her hand and slid his hand up to cup her cheek and then moved it behind her head, pulling her down closer so that he could look her in the eyes.

"I was someone you would not want to know. I was the nightmare you tell children about."

"I know who you are Jeremiah Silverman, and you are none of those things."

He shook his head. "You don't understand, but you will. That's not even my name."

He tried to lift his other hand to touch her face and pain roared through him.

She pulled away. "You're in pain, you're hallucinating. Here, take this."

She handed him a couple of pills.

He didn't want to take them, but the pain was starting to make him dizzy. He popped them in his mouth and then took the water glass she handed him.

He downed the pills, and handed her the glass. She put it back on the nightstand and then stood. "Is there anything else I can get you?" she asked.

He stared at her, his vision growing fuzzy. She didn't want to know. It was his burden to carry, not hers. And so it would remain.

He watched her walk out of the room and then he fell asleep again.

Cindy lay back down on the couch, her heart pounding so hard she thought it was going to burst. Jeremiah had been incoherent. He was clearly trying to talk to her, but she'd made out very little of it. It had been hard to concentrate with her hand on his chest. She had felt all the scar tissue there and she had felt so much pain and grief for what he must have been through. The only thing that had been really clear was that he seemed to have gotten one of the knife wounds while training in hand-to-hand combat.

He had been struggling so hard to tell her something, but whether it was about his time in the army or not she didn't know. She would have listened all night, but he was in pain and he needed rest more than anything.

And when he was ready to tell her whatever he had felt so burdened to tell her he would. Until then she'd just have to be patient and not push too much. It was clear that his life had been painful and that was something she could understand. She had never even told him the full story about what happened to her sister.

She took a ragged breath. All she knew was that she cared for him deeply. Maybe too deeply. She closed her eyes and tried to force herself to go to sleep.

Jeremiah woke in the morning to the smell of something cooking. He sat up slowly, feeling a little woozy still, but on the whole much better than he had been. He stood and made his way to the bathroom then a minute later walked into the kitchen.

Cindy was standing over the oven, making what looked like omelets. Captain was laying at her feet, clearly hoping for a handout. The overhead lights were reflecting off Cindy's hair and he froze as the events of the middle of the night came back to him.

Fear flooded through him. The things he had said. And now he'd have to face the consequences of it. He wasn't ready for this. She had rejected him last night, rejected what he had to say. Hadn't she? That's the way it had seemed.

Yet here she was, making breakfast in his kitchen. Everything was such a blur, he couldn't know for sure what he had actually said.

"It smells good," he forced himself to say.

She looked up with a smile. "Thanks. You look better."

"I feel better," he admitted, moving to lean against one of the counters.

"Different clothes," he noticed suddenly. She wasn't wearing what she had been the night before.

"Geanie dropped these off for me a while ago along with the food," she said.

"Remind me to thank her."

"This is just about ready if you want to sit," she said.

He nodded and headed to his dining table. He had been sitting less than a minute when she brought in two plates. She set them down and returned a moment later with utensils and two glasses of orange juice.

"Wow, what a feast," he said, suddenly very aware that he was only half-dressed.

"Breakfast of champions," she said brightly.

He started to eat. He was pretty sure it tasted good, but his mind was preoccupied with other things.

"Thanks for staying last night," he said. "I know that had to be a...burden."

"No, it was fine," she said, smiling again.

She was doing a lot of that. Was it genuine or was it for his benefit?

They finished their breakfast in silence and then he went to get changed while she cleaned up. He glanced at his clock and moved as quickly as he could. He needed to get to the synagogue and get the day started.

He managed to take care of everything except the buttons on his shirt. He finally gave up in frustration and walked back into the kitchen where Cindy was just finishing up.

She turned. "You managed pretty well for a guy who was shot last night."

"You know us rabbis, take a licking, keep on ticking," he said. "I figure I've seen worse."

She didn't say anything. She wasn't giving him any indication of exactly what had happened last night from her perspective. He didn't want to come right out and ask her, though, in case his memories were accurate and she had rejected wanting to know more about his past.

"Here, do you need some help?" she asked after drying her hands on a dish towel.

"Sorry."

"It's okay," she said.

She walked over and grabbed the edges of his shirt. He could feel her fingers brush his chest and the sensory input reminded him so strongly of the night before that it was all he could do to stand still and say nothing.

"This is harder to do for someone else than you'd think," she laughed after fumbling with the first button and finally getting it through the hole.

"I can imagine," he said.

Her touch was like torture. He found himself wanting to burst out his confession then and there. But not for nothing had he gone so long undetected.

Finally he had to say something. It was becoming unnatural. "I'm sorry you had to see my scars," he said.

She shook her head. "I'm sorry you have them. I can't imagine what you must have gone through in the army. It must have hurt so much when your training partner stabbed you."

He caught her hands in his and she looked up and met his eyes.

His heart was pounding. "I said that last night?" he asked.

She nodded. "You said a lot of things."

"Like what?" he whispered.

Her brow furrowed. "I honestly don't know. You were raving quite a lot. I think you might have been hallucinating. It was clear you had something important you wanted to tell me, but of everything you said, most of it was babble. That was the only thing I could actually make out. The scar over your ribs was from when you were learning hand-to-hand combat."

"I'm sorry you had to hear that," he said, tightening his grip and continuing to stare into her eyes.

"No, it's fine. Whatever you want to tell me. Whenever you want to tell me. It's okay. I'm not going anywhere."

She was telling the truth. He forced himself to keep his face from reflecting his relief. He had not debased himself in her eyes.

"Thank you," he said, and dropped her hands.

"You're welcome," she responded as she continued to button his shirt.

Ten minutes later they were in Cindy's car heading to work. He stared out the window, lost in thought. She seemed content to be silent as well. Finally they pulled up outside her church.

He slowly got out of the car and she did the same.

"Thanks for the ride," he said. It sounded so lame, but he couldn't think of anything else to say.

"Are you sure you don't want me to walk in with you?" she asked.

"No, I don't need to give Marie more reason to fuss. I'm hoping I can even avoid her finding out I got shot last night," Jeremiah said.

"Is that why you're not wearing the sling?" she asked.

"You've got it. A little physical pain is far easier to deal with than one of her tirades. Especially today."

Cindy shook her head, but didn't say anything.

"Thank you, again."

"I'm next door if you need anything," she said.

"I'll do my best to leave you in peace today. Besides, I'm going to be so preoccupied with synagogue business that I seriously doubt anything else will be coming up to distract me," he said.

At least, he certainly hoped so. He couldn't help but remember the touch of her fingers on his chest as she'd buttoned his shirt. He didn't want to think about it. That led to thinking about how he almost kissed her before. And that was something he was most certainly not thinking of. At least, not until he and G-d could have a good long discussion about this past year and the next one.

He smiled, glad that she couldn't read his thoughts. She'd probably be horrified if she could.

He watched as she walked onto the church campus. Then he turned and headed to the synagogue.

His office was the last place Jeremiah wanted to be, but he needed to go in. It was only a few hours until the start of Rosh Hashanah and he had too much to do to waste time. When he walked in the door Marie looked like she was preparing to give him the lecture of his life. Something in his expression must have given her pause, though, since she held her tongue. It was an act of mercy that he appreciated, especially since he was in no mood to try and curb his response.

He grimaced in greeting, walked over to his office, unlocked it and stepped inside closing the door behind him. His eyes fell on the package that had come several days ago that he had completely forgotten about until that moment.

A terrible suspicion flooded him as he stared at the brown wrapped package.

"It couldn't be," he whispered.

He sat down on the couch and pulled the package close. It did feel like some sort of painting. He balanced it with his left hand, biting his lip against the fire that burned through his arm at the movement and tore off the paper with his right.

He saw the back of the painting first, already prepped and ready for mounting. There was a string of letters and numbers on the back written in black ink and below it another set of numbers written in blue ink. He spun it around slowly and as he saw what it was his heart stuttered.

"You have got to be kidding me!"

Mark was sitting at his desk wondering how he was even managing to be conscious given how little sleep he'd gotten. He picked up his cup of coffee and took a swig.

"Mark!"

He jerked and splashed coffee all over his jacket. He winced and grabbed a couple of sticky notes and tried to sop some of it up as he looked up to see who had called him.

Liam was weaving his way toward him waving the camera in his hand. He had a huge grin on his face and, worse, he looked fully rested. Mark couldn't help but hate him at that moment.

Liam set the camera down on the desk. "I finished up last night."

"That must have taken forever," Mark muttered as he stood up and swiped some tissues off a neighboring desk. He blotted his jacket some more and then gave up and took it off. He hung it on the back of his chair with a sigh. He'd just gotten that one back from the cleaners, too.

"It wasn't too bad as long as I didn't have to be on the ladder," Liam said.

"Good. I'll make sure it gets to the rabbi today."

"Don't forget that Rosh Hashanah starts at sundown tonight. Once that happens you won't get anything out of him for at least a couple of days. Maybe longer."

"Thanks for the warning, reminder, whatever it was," Mark said, as he rubbed his eyes.

"What's on your docket for today?" Liam asked eagerly.

"Mostly today is going to be sitting on top of lab guys trying to get test results, answers, something I can actually work with. Fingerprints, DNA, someone to tell me whether or not that piece of the Amber Room we found in the house is authentic or just some kook's idea of a joke. You?"

Liam's face fell slightly. "Patrol."

"Sorry, I forgot for a second," Mark said.

That seemed to cheer Liam back up.

Once he'd gone Mark stared at the piece of paper in front of him, trying to decide what to tackle first. It was going to be a boring day, but that was good. He'd had about as much excitement as he could handle.

Jeremiah yanked his cell phone out of his pocket and called Mark.

"What is it?" the detective asked without preamble. He sounded half asleep and none too thrilled to be disturbed.

"I've got something at my office you're going to want to see," Jeremiah said and then hung up. Next he dialed Cindy.

"How are you feeling?" she asked, sounding mildly alarmed. "Is everything okay?"

"Okay, but I have something at my office you're going to have to see to believe," he said.

She paused. "The last time you said something like that you'd torn up the floor and found, you know, what you found," she said, lowering her voice.

He took it that there was someone nearby that she didn't want overhearing.

"Well I have something else pretty amazing," he said.

"Is it, you know, another piece of the same thing?" she asked, sounding perplexed.

"No, it's not another piece of the Amber Room, but you're on the right track. Just, come and take a look."

"Hold on a sec."

She put the phone down and he could hear her moving around then silence. About a minute later she picked the phone back up. "I need ten minutes and then I'll be right over," she said.

She hung up and Jeremiah stood and began pacing the room. He stopped and checked the back of the painting again, paying particular attention to the letters and numbers in black ink. KF114. He got his phone back out and took a couple of pictures of the back then took a couple of pictures of the painting itself.

Next he went over to his computer and did a quick search, just to make sure he was right about what it was he was staring at. In thirty seconds he knew that he was.

His arm was beginning to really throb so he took some Tylenol. He wasn't about to risk another round with whatever the doctor had prescribed that had knocked him out so hard the night before.

This would explain everything that had been going on, or rather, a good deal of it. He could barely contain himself anymore and he yanked open his office door, startling Marie who looked up at him like he had gone mad.

"Something wrong?" she asked.

"No, I just think I figured something out about the case I'm helping the detective with," Jeremiah said. There was no need to put her in danger by bringing her into the loop. The less she knew at this point, the safer she was.

"Are you sure you're okay? You're white as a sheet," she clucked.

"I'm just tired," he said.

"You better get some sleep before you have to do any of the liturgy," she said.

"Yes, that would be a brilliant idea," he said.

"Now I know there's something wrong," he heard Marie mutter.

Sylvia graciously allowed Cindy to lock up the office and put a "back in fifteen minutes" sign on the front door. With Geanie gone, it was harder to do anything because it was just her working in the main office and she couldn't leave it unlocked. It was hard just to grab a soda when she wanted one.

She was going to have to find a way to get Geanie to agree to come back to work. She'd only been gone a couple of days and already some of the other staff and ministry leaders were freaking out. And she was going to personally freak out if they expected her to take over Geanie's responsibilities while they found a replacement.

She was feeling worse every minute she was there. She wasn't sure if it was just anxiety or if everything was catching up to her. Geanie was right, she should have called in sick.

As she headed over to the synagogue she couldn't help but wonder what it was that Jeremiah had found. If it wasn't another piece of the Amber Room, maybe it was another painting. But that didn't make any sense either. What would something like that be doing in his office?

He must have looked something up online and found new information. That made a lot more sense. She had just made it to the synagogue parking lot when a familiar car pulled up.

"Hey, Mark," she called as he got out of the car.

"He called you, too?"

"Yeah. Must be important if he's hauling us both over here. I just can't figure out what it could be. I dropped him off at work like twenty minutes ago."

"I don't know, but it better be good. I feel like the walking dead."

"You look somewhat like a zombie," she said.

"Nice. Thanks for the affirmation."

They walked into the office and Marie looked up from her desk. Cindy felt like the woman was glaring daggers at her. She forced herself to smile in return.

"He's been expecting you," Marie said to Mark.

The detective nodded and together they entered Jeremiah's office. Mark closed the door behind them.

"You made it," Jeremiah said, looking more excited than Cindy had ever seen him.

"Yup, and I brought a little present for you," Mark said, putting a video camera he'd been holding down on Jeremiah's desk. "I had Liam videotape the rest of the writing on those walls so that when you have a few moments you can continue with the translation work. Hopefully it will be easier on everyone this way."

Jeremiah barely even glanced at the video camera before scooping it up and putting it next to his computer monitor. He turned back to them.

"Okay, so we're both here, what is it?" Mark asked.

Cindy noticed that there was a painting leaning against the couch. She could only see the back of it where some letters and numbers had been written in ink.

Jeremiah turned it around and she stared at it.

It looked like a classical piece, like some she had seen in a museum somewhere. In the center of the piece was a naked woman standing next to a seated man with a long beard who was looking at her. Beneath the woman's feet it looked like two human figures were being swallowed by the ground or the water, she struggled to make it all out. To the left of the man a lion and a tiger were snapping at each other. Behind them was what looked like a man carrying something and to the far edge a rhinoceros. To the right of the woman was something that she at first took to be a gorilla but on closer inspection seemed to resemble a hippopotamus more.

"Okay, not something I'd necessarily care to see hanging in a rabbi's office, or in any church office for that matter," Mark said.

"Half the churches in Italy seem to be covered with nude paintings. It was the style," Cindy said. "Not that I see it being hung in a church here, either."

Jeremiah looked both excited and impatient at the same time.

"Do you know what this is?" he asked.

Both Cindy and Mark shook their heads.

"Well, I can tell it's a painting, but beyond that...okay, I'll bite. What is it?" Mark asked.

Jeremiah took a deep breath. "It's a Rubens. Neptune and Amphitrite."

Cindy blinked. She didn't know a lot about art, but even she'd heard the name Rubens before.

"He was one of the masters," Jeremiah continued.

Mark and Cindy stared at each other and then back at the painting.

"Is it real or a reproduction?" Cindy asked at last.

"Until a couple of days ago I would have said it absolutely had to be a reproduction."

She ogled the painting. That was certainly a bigger find than her dogs playing poker.

"Why is that? What makes you think it was real when before you wouldn't have?" Mark asked.

"Because this painting was supposedly destroyed, along with over 400 others, in Friedrichshain Flakturm in Berlin in 1945."

Mark whistled.

"What is a Flakturm?" Cindy asked, after a moment.

"They were anti-aircraft gun towers that also served as bomb shelters," Mark offered.

Jeremiah glanced at Mark in surprise.

Mark shrugged. "My grandfather fought in WWII, came home and became an architect. He was like a walking encyclopedia about German architecture. Some of it stuck. The more important question here is how did you come by it."

"That's the thing," Jeremiah said. "It was here the morning that you called me over to see the writing on the walls. I had just gotten in and Marie told me someone had left a package that she'd found when she got to work. You called, I put it in my office, and I forgot completely about it until I got in today.

"I saw it and I immediately thought of the painting Cindy found. I also thought about Heinrich wanting to talk to me three months ago and never following up. When I opened it and realized what I was looking at I called both of you."

Cindy bent down to take a closer look. She reached out hesitantly and touched the frame. If it was real, it was the closest she would come to actually being able to touch a famous piece of art in her lifetime.

"But how do you know this isn't a copy of some sort?" Cindy asked.

"Someone was bound to want to recreate it if they could," Mark said.

"You can find pictures of it online that were taken before it was destroyed so that copies could be distributed in books and for students to study. I'm sure there's more than one reproduction out there," Jeremiah said. "We're going to need an expert to authenticate it, but I found something that convinces me, at least."

"What's that?" Mark asked.

Jeremiah flipped the painting around. He pointed to the first written line which was in black ink. "You see this top line of writing here on the back, KF114?"

"Yes," Mark said.

"Does it mean something?" Cindy asked.

"When the Nazis stole artwork from Jewish families, they'd catalogue it in this way. First a letter that stood for the first letter in the family's last name, then a number indicating which piece this was in the collection. This piece was part of the Kaiser Friedrich Museum in Berlin. It was moved to the Flakturm where it was hoped it would be kept safe. However, the Flakturm suffered two successive fires and the pieces housed inside were believed to be destroyed. Whoever moved this from the Flakturm where it was being housed followed the Nazi naming system. The KF stands for Kaiser Friedrich and this is the 114th piece taken."

Cindy blinked. "If this one is marked 114, does that mean that at least 113 other pieces were also taken from the Flakturm before it was burned? Maybe even more?"

Jeremiah nodded. "That would be my guess."

"If that's true, and Heinrich left this for you hours before he died, then this guy could have known where a fortune was hidden. 114 paintings or more. What are we talking, millions of dollars?" Mark asked.

"Hundreds of millions of dollars," Jeremiah said. "There was more than one Rubens in that group and if they're among the ones that were saved..." he didn't bother completing the thought. "And it's more than just money at this point, it's restoring masterpieces thought lost. I'd almost say that at this point they're priceless."

"Who do they belong to?" Mark asked.

"That's a good question," Jeremiah said. "I believe the collection, or at least part of it, was legitimately owned by the museum. They probably belong to Germany."

"But I'm sure there's a whole lot of people who would like to contest that," Mark said, looking more and more flustered.

Jeremiah shrugged.

Cindy's mind boggled at the number. She took a step back from the painting, not wanting to be the one to mar it if it was authentic.

Jeremiah's adrenalin was starting to wear off a little and the pain in his arm wasn't receding as fast as he'd like it to. He was gratified at both Mark and Cindy's reactions. Of course, that didn't detract from the fact that they had a big problem on their hands now when it came to figuring out what to do with this thing. There were a dozen different ways they could go, plays that could be made. Part of the problem was they didn't yet know who all the actors involved in this drama were, not by a long shot.

It complicated things. His eyes strayed to Cindy and he watched her as she stared at the painting, clearly overwhelmed by everything. Complicated was the last thing he needed right now in his life.

It was certainly the last thing that she needed in hers.

More things were beginning to trouble him about this case and he didn't have the time to properly think about them. It did seem odd that Heinrich would have left this on his doorstep mere hours before he was killed. Why?

He was also becoming more and more suspicious about the true nature of the poker playing dog painting. It was not unheard of for art thieves to paint over a more famous painting with something mundane. An art restorer could easily strip off the new paint at a later date without damaging the original.

But why would Heinrich go to all the trouble of hiding the identity of that painting, but not this one? None of that made sense. There was clearly a missing piece of the puzzle.

He looked again at the back of the painting with its mounting brackets in place. He found himself wondering if this had been the lone painting on Heinrich's dining room wall that the single nail hole hinted had been present.

Whatever was happening, the implications could be staggering. With only a few hours before the holiday started, he realized that he couldn't be the one to pursue any of this as much as he'd like to.

He took a deep breath. It was time to relinquish responsibility for all of this. "Well, Detective, what do you want to do?" he asked.

Mark passed a hand over his face. "Hundreds of millions of dollars in art, the Amber Room, two dead art restorers, a dead Nazi, a dog painting stolen from a police car, and someone in a car with diplomatic plates taking a shot at you. Even if the picture is a reproduction, and the slab of wall is fake, this is getting too big, too crazy. We need to call in the F.B.I. or somebody. I just need to slow down and think for a moment. This is way bigger than anything I've ever even heard of before if it's all true."

"What do you think?" Cindy asked, turning to look at Jeremiah.

"About what?" he asked.

"About what we should do? Do you think Mark should call the F.B.I.?"

It wasn't good that she was automatically deferring to him instead of Mark on a question like that. He opened his mouth to respond, to tell her that he thought they should leave the decision making to Mark. After all, they were civilians just along for the ride.

Before he could say anything, Jeremiah heard the sound of the main office door slam. No one ever slammed the door like that, not even Marie. He felt the hair on the back of his neck rise and he was overcome with a sudden distinct uneasiness.

Maybe he was being paranoid, but what about the last few days hadn't gone completely awry? A moment later he heard a startled exclamation from Marie which was enough to turn his blood to ice water in his veins.

"I think we're all in a lot of trouble," he said eyes darting around the room, as he snatched up the painting.

"What are you doing?" Cindy asked as Jeremiah yanked open the closet in his office and threw the painting up onto the top shelf. He snatched a coat off of a hangar inside and tossed it over the painting.

"Sit!" he hissed, waving to the couch as he dropped into his chair behind his desk and leaned forward, face solemn.

Cindy sat and after a moment Mark did as well, looking nearly as puzzled as she felt.

Jeremiah cleared his throat and spoke up in a loud voice, "Now, look you two, I know that marriage is hard, but you have to try and work it out. I'm tired of hearing about your petty squabbles."

"What-" Mark began.

Jeremiah held up his hand. "Don't interrupt! Now I want each of you to look at the other and tell that person sitting next to you that you still love them."

Cindy wondered if Jeremiah was hallucinating from the medication the doctors had put him on. That had to be the only explanation for what he was doing.

"Do it, now!" Jeremiah demanded.

She jumped at the intensity of his tone and timidly turned to Mark who was now looking more frightened than puzzled.

"Hold hands while you do it," Jeremiah instructed.

Nervously, awkwardly, Mark reached out and took Cindy's hands in his. His touch made her jump again.

"Good, now tell her you love her," Jeremiah told Mark.

"Cindy, I uh, well, you know how I feel-"

"Not good enough!"

"Please, this isn't necessary," Cindy burst out.

"It is. Telling your spouse you love them is the most necessary thing to a healthy marriage. Now tell her," he said.

"Cindy," Mark said, his eyes pleading with her to figure out what was going on, "I-I love you."

The door flew open, startling both of them.

Jeremiah turned and barked. "I'm in the middle of a marriage counseling session. Make an appointment with my secretary."

"It can't wait," a man with a thick German accent said.

Cindy saw Mark's eyes widen in comprehension. He turned around toward the door. "Look, if you don't mind, my wife and I were just having a moment."

"This will only take a moment, I assure you," the speaker said.

Cindy glanced at him. He was in his fifties with salt and pepper hair, pale skin, thin lips, and shifty looking eyes.

Jeremiah stood up and moved toward the door. "I'm sorry, but this is unacceptable. Marie!"

"I'm afraid my associate has her busy at the moment. Allow me to introduce myself. My name is Albert Schmidt. I work for the German consulate in Los Angeles. I'm attempting to clear up a few...irregularities let us say regarding one of our citizens who was residing in this area until recently. Heinrich Beck. I believe you know him?"

Cindy felt her spine stiffen and she turned back to Mark who was carefully avoiding catching the eye of the

German. He was squeezing her hands hard now, hard enough that it hurt, but she didn't dare move a muscle. She had no idea what Jeremiah had in mind, but she sensed that somehow he had known something was about to happen. That would explain his hiding the painting and his subsequent strange behavior.

"I never met the man," Jeremiah lied coolly, "but I've been in his home. I was called in to try and interpret some Hebrew writing that was found there. It's a mess, though, mostly gibberish with an occasional word. It's worse than trying to read a five-year-old's scribblings if all they knew was pig Latin. Whoever left the writing clearly didn't learn Hebrew from a qualified teacher. It was a complete waste of time and I'm happy to be done with that. Now, if you could tell me if there's anything you need quickly, I'd appreciate it. I need to finish up with this couple and then I have to make preparations for the start of Rosh Hashanah this evening."

"I just wanted to give you my card and tell you that if you found anything...unusual...in his writings, particularly relating to belongings, a will, anything like that I'd appreciate hearing. His grandchildren are quite concerned about some personal property of his that no one can seem to locate."

Cindy saw Jeremiah take the card. "Frankly, I didn't find anything like that. I don't have any plans to return to the house. This is my busiest time of year and I'm going to be completely taken up with work for the next three weeks. I'll keep your card, though, in case I hear something, though it's unlikely."

"I...appreciate it," Albert said, his voice ominous to Cindy's ears.

"Good luck with your marriage. You should listen to the rabbi. 'I love you' is the most powerful thing a couple can say to one another."

He turned and walked out the door. Jeremiah shut it behind him and then leaned his ear against it, clearly listening.

Cindy pulled her hands away and Mark let them go with an apologetic grimace. He stood and drew his gun, clearly waiting for some sort of signal from Jeremiah.

She wondered where the most out of the way place for her to be was and decided that there truly wasn't a good spot in the office for her to be. She pulled her feet as close to the couch as possible and got ready to move at a moment's notice.

Another minute crawled by in absolute silence and then Jeremiah's shoulders relaxed. He opened the door and strode out into the main office.

"Are you okay?" she heard him asking Marie.

"Who were those dreadful men?" she heard his secretary ask.

"They're from the German consulate," he said. "What did they ask you?"

"They asked me if Heinrich Beck had ever come by here or given you or me anything. I told them I had never even heard of Heinrich Beck."

"Good," Jeremiah said, then started to walk back into his office.

"Who is Heinrich Beck?" Marie called after him.

"A dead man," he said over his shoulder.

He closed the door and sat down on the edge of his desk as Mark reholstered his weapon.

"That was pretty tricky, Rabbi," Mark said.

"How did you know?" Cindy asked.

"I heard the door slam and the way Marie reacted it sounded like it was a stranger. She would have lit into them for slamming the door if it was someone she knew. Given everything that's happened, I made an educated guess."

"You saved our butts with that guess," Mark said. "I just can't believe it worked."

"Do you think that was the man who shot you?" Cindy asked, feeling sick to her stomach even as she asked.

"He's certainly capable of shooting someone and he was wearing a gun in a holster," Jeremiah said. "Something tells me, though, that he wasn't the one who shot me."

"Pardon me if I kind of hope you're wrong about that one," Mark said. "Because if you're right, that's one more person involved that we don't know about. I guess it could be someone else at the consulate."

"Maybe, maybe not," Jeremiah said. "After all, when the paintings were thought destroyed, the Russians were occupying Berlin. It's possible that a Russian had a hand in stealing those paintings, payback for the Amber Room, spoils of war, something."

"Then how would Heinrich have gotten involved? Wouldn't it have been more likely for this hypothetical Russian to involve other Russians instead of a German?"

"Perhaps. Perhaps Heinrich was easier to work with, or in the right place, or he thought about getting rid of him afterward. Then again, maybe it's the Russians or someone else who figured out after all this time that

Heinrich had access to these things and has come looking."

"Do you know there's like 150 consulates in Los Angeles," Mark said with a groan. "This could end up being a very large haystack we're looking in."

"Odds are good, though, it's one of the European ones involved, those are the countries that have been most active in tracking the missing art pieces from the war."

"Still, that's a lot of consulates and it's not like we can just waltz in and start questioning their people."

"You're right about one thing," Jeremiah said. "This is all getting very complicated very quickly."

"I'm not sure my nerves can take much more," Cindy admitted. Now that the danger was over she realized she was starting to shake. Embarrassed, she folded her hands in her lap, hoping neither of them noticed.

"I know a guy in the Bureau. I'm going to give him a call. Hopefully we can manage this a bit so whoever they send our way won't be a total jerk," Mark said.

"Sounds like a good idea," Jeremiah said. He took a deep breath. "What I told that guy was true. Rosh Hashanah starts in just a few hours and I have to be able to focus on that. I can't let down my congregation. I'm out of time to work on this whole problem."

"And I'm out of names of art restorers. I'm going to have to find someone we can trust who might not already be in the crosshairs for whoever took out the last one," Mark said. "Maybe my friend can recommend someone in the Bureau for that, too."

"Maybe your killer won't be looking for their next target now that they have the painting that you had."

"Or maybe they're going to go all kinds of crazy looking for the one that you now have," Mark said.

Cindy was getting a headache, but she didn't want to just leave. "What are you going to do with that painting?" she asked.

Mark and Jeremiah looked at each other.

"I'm going to be here all day," Jeremiah said. "I think I can find a better hiding place for it until you find someplace safe to take it."

"That sounds like a good plan to me," Mark said. "Clearly my car isn't the place to keep it." He rolled his eyes in disgust.

"So, that's settled. I'll hide it. You'll look for someone who can authenticate it."

"And I'll get back to work," Cindy said, dragging herself up off the couch.

"I'll walk out with you, make sure those guys aren't still lurking around," Mark said.

"Good idea," Jeremiah told him.

"Just don't hold my hand again. I'm going to be bruised from the last time," she said.

Mark grinned at her.

It wasn't a joke, she thought, but she didn't bother telling him that.

She was grateful, though, as they walked out of the office that he was with her. This way if those creeps were still around she would be safer than if she was alone.

As it turned out they were nowhere to be seen and neither the synagogue nor the church parking lot had any strange cars, certainly no black ones with darkened windows.

Mark was a gentleman and walked her onto the church campus and up to the door of her office.

"Thanks," she told him.

"Anytime," he said, then turned to go.

She took a deep breath before opening the door, trying to get herself back into a work frame of mind. Cindy walked into the office and stopped midstride. Sylvia, the business manager, was seated at her desk, staring off into space.

"Sylvia? What's going on?" Cindy asked.

The older woman looked up. "Royus."

Cindy's heart sank. "What are they doing now?"

"They're in my office going over the budget. Gus wants more money for the Christmas production and Roy doesn't think there's any way he can have it."

"What do you think?" Cindy asked.

"Does it matter?"

"Well, you are the business manager. It is your job to handle the money. Shouldn't they be asking you instead of trying to argue it out themselves?"

"You would think," Sylvia said, with an eerie calm to her voice. "They originally came into my office wanting to know how soon before I could have another graphic designer in here."

Cindy felt sick at the very thought of someone else sitting at Geanie's desk. "What did you tell them?"

She shrugged. "I didn't get a chance to tell them I wasn't planning on hiring anyone for at least a month. Probably just as well. I'm not sure either of them could have handled that answer."

"If they both weren't acting like such idiots, they wouldn't have to wait for you to hire a new graphic designer," Cindy growled.

"Too true. Good luck getting them to see that, though."

A quiet fire seemed to be building inside of Cindy. It wasn't right that Gus and Roy's feud was doing so much damage to the rest of them. She thought of poor Dave and wondered how soon before he quit. When that happened it would be a black day for the church, and the kids would be devastated. It wasn't right. She was about sick to death of things that weren't right.

Sylvia got up. "Sorry, I took your desk. I needed to make a phone call and my office was...occupied."

"It's okay," Cindy said, moving around it and sitting down.

Sylvia glanced at her and frowned. "Are you okay?"

Cindy self-consciously put her hands under her desk and faked a smile. "Just tired and a bit stressed, I guess."

Sylvia sat down in the chair in front of Cindy's desk. "You need to take better care of yourself," she said.

"I try to," Cindy said sheepishly. Having Sylvia talk to her felt a bit like having a mother talk to her. The only difference was, Sylvia cared more about her welfare than her own mom seemed to. Maybe it was because Sylvia didn't have any kids of her own.

"I'm not just talking the clichés here like good food, plenty of rest, and exercise."

"Yeah, because last time I tried to go on vacation it worked out so well," Cindy said, the sarcasm slipping out. She bit her lip. "I'm sorry, I'm just tired."

"Don't be sorry. You're being honest. That's a good thing. You don't have to pretend with me, you know. I like honest, even when it's messy and unpleasant and harsh."

Cindy shook her head. "Three words I definitely don't enjoy."

Sylvia shrugged. "I'm just saying, let yourself go through what you're going through, don't judge yourself, don't even try to pretend for other people. In the end it will just exhaust you and end up taking you three times as long to work through what you need to. If you need a mental health day, you take it. You need to punch something, sign up to a real gym."

Cindy wasn't sure whether to be amused or embarrassed. "Did someone tell you that I slapped Jeremiah?"

"No, but I'm guessing he had it coming. I'd rather you hit a punching bag than a man, but at least you let something out."

"Thanks."

"Don't thank me. I had a terrible childhood, the kind they make movies about that make everyone cry and vow to be better people. I learned the hard way that if you don't learn to care for yourself, you'll never heal, never grow, never learn how to really live. So much of our lives are spent putting on a brave face and being strong for other people, whether it's out of guilt or shame or a misplaced sense of responsibility. Let yourself grieve, let yourself rage, whatever it is you need to do, do it. And don't apologize to anyone for it."

"Thanks, I'll try to remember that," Cindy said.

Sylvia stood. "I'll be here to remind you if I need to. Now it's time I go kick those two out of my office so I can get some work done."

Sylvia made a certain amount of sense, but it sounded easier said than done. Cindy had spent so much of her life afraid, and just as much of her life hiding that fear from other people.

She shook her head. Time to grieve or rage or whatever later. Now it was time to get back to work. She glanced at the clock. It was ten in the morning. She sighed. Only seven more hours until she could go home and get busy trying to do something else.

Mark headed back to the office. Once there he put in a call to his friend Vince, at the bureau.

"What on earth has got me accepting a call from you this early in the morning?" Vince asked in a friendly tone.

"A heck of a mess," Mark admitted.

"How about you give me a preview?" Vince said with a laugh.

Ten minutes later Vince wasn't laughing anymore. "That is seriously messed up all the way around," he said.

"I told you."

"You did the right thing calling. I know a couple of agents to sic on this. Can you send me over some files?"

"I'll fax you what I've got as soon as I'm off the phone," Mark promised.

"Okay. I'll take a look and then get them started on them. I wouldn't expect a call back until tomorrow probably."

"As long as no one else gets shot in the meantime I'm okay with that."

"I miss your sense of humor. Tell you what, I'll try to find you someone who can do some art authentication right away."

"I would appreciate that. The longer we're in the dark the harder it is to keep from tripping over stuff."

After they hung up Mark faxed him the file. Then he debated his next move. Before he could make a decision he got a text on his phone from Vince.

Sorry, no number. Your art guy is Joe Weinstein.

There was an address in Los Angeles.

Great, Mark thought with a grimace. Driving into Los Angeles was exactly what he didn't want to do. Oh well, maybe he'd manage to cruise by a couple of consulates while he was at it. Not that he could even dare go inside and start asking questions. And he was sure it was too much to hope that they'd have black cars sitting out front that he could take pictures of and send to Cindy and Jeremiah to try and identify, but one could dream.

Several hours later he realized the whole thing had been one ridiculous dream. He'd spent three hours getting to his first destination, what should have been a one hour trip, but there were accidents on multiple freeways in the city. He'd made it to the art guy's place just to find that it was a house, not a business, and no one seemed to be home. He left his card stuck in the front door with a note on the back to call him.

Then he spent a couple of hours just trying to drive by the German and Russian embassies. As expected, no ominous black cars hanging around. Finally he gave up, realizing that most of the day was pretty much a bust. From the sounds of things on the radio, traffic was going to be even worse getting back out of the city. Just one more reason he hated L.A.

He called Traci. "I'm in L.A. I'll be home for dinner...whenever I can get there."

"Okay," she said. "You must be in a good mood."

"You know how much I love the city."

"Then I'll make sure to make something yummy for dinner."

"You are the best," he said.

He hung up and felt himself grin. He might be trapped in bumper-to-bumper traffic for a few hours but at least he had a wonderful wife to get home to.

Cindy was running on fumes. She glanced at the clock on the wall. It was four-forty. Only twenty minutes left.

You can do it, she told herself, *just hang in there*.

The rest of her day had been crazy hectic. With Geanie not there everyone had been suddenly looking to her to figure out what to do about the programs for Sunday services. She had thought on three separate occasions that it might just be her day to quit her job.

She had gotten through, though, somehow. Now she was just hoping for a few minutes of calm while she wrapped things up.

The door opened and she winced, not wanting to have to deal with anyone else.

She glanced up, expecting to see one of the staff or ministry leaders. Instead a man and a woman, both wearing black suits and white shirts walked in. They both walked with a sense of purpose.

They headed straight for her desk and she felt herself tensing up as she wondered who they were and what they wanted.

"Cindy Preston?" the man asked.

"Yes?" she asked.

He pulled out a badge. "Agent Davies, F.B.I. You need to come with us. Right now."

Mark had been going to call in the F.B.I. and she couldn't help but wonder if something else happened to him or Jeremiah. "Why, what's wrong?" she asked, standing up as anxiety began to course through her. She could feel her hands starting to shake again.

"You're under arrest for grand larceny, smuggling, and conspiracy to commit murder."

"What?" Cindy asked, struggling to process what Agent Davies had just said.

"Ma'am, turn around and put your hands behind your back," he said.

She stared at him, wondering what on earth he was doing.

"Ma'am, don't make us ask you again," the female agent said, her hand moving under her jacket and touching the barely visible butt of a gun.

"Th-this is a mistake," Cindy stuttered.

Davies produced a pair of handcuffs, put his hand on her shoulder and spun her around. He yanked her right arm behind her and she cried out in pain. Cold steel snapped tight around her wrist.

"What are you doing?" she cried.

He grabbed her other arm and in a moment she was completely handcuffed. He spun her back around. "You're coming with us. You have a lot to answer for."

"This is a mistake. Call Detective Mark Walters, he'll tell you. I don't know what you've heard, but I'm one of the good guys."

"That's what they all say," the woman sneered.

"I'm innocent!" Cindy shouted. "Why won't you listen to me! Call Mark, he'll tell you what's going on. I'm helping him."

"More like helping yourself," Davies said.

Fear and pain mixed together inside her and she felt like an explosion waiting to happen. She wanted to scream, cry, kick, fight, whatever it took.

The door opened before they reached it and Roy walked in. "What's going on here?" he demanded.

"F.B.I.," the woman said, flashing her badge. "We've placed this woman under arrest."

"Oh, oh, I see," he said, looking stunned at first. Then he turned and looked Cindy in the eyes. Instead of compassion, she saw condemnation there as his lips tightened into a thin line. He opened the door for the officers and they pushed her out of it.

"Help me!" she screamed. "Call Detective Mark Walters! Tell him what's happening! They've got the wrong person! Call Jeremiah! Tell them it's Agent Davies and his partner!"

She looked around frantically, hoping to see Sylvia or Dave. They would help. She screamed at the top of her lungs, hoping it would bring someone else running.

The two agents just pushed her along faster. She tripped but Davies who was holding her by her upper arm kept her on her feet and half dragged her forward.

"I didn't do anything," she sobbed.

"Cut the crap, we all know you're guilty," Davies growled. "Protesting won't do you any good here. We have proof."

"What proof?" she sobbed.

Her entire body was shaking uncontrollably now and she realized she was going to throw up. When they made it to the parking lot, she doubled over and retched. As soon as she was finished, they shoved her into the back of a black van. She fell onto the seat, blood roaring in her ears and she blacked out.

When she came to she was sitting in a gray room in one of three chairs at a table. The two chairs across from her sat vacant. Overhead florescent lights hummed, the only sound in the silence.

Her hands were still handcuffed together, but now they were in front of her body instead of behind it. Also, the cuffs weren't cutting as deeply into her wrists as they had been before. She supposed she should be grateful for the small things, but her mind was too filled with panic over what was happening to her.

Had someone heard her at the church and called Mark or Jeremiah? Were they right now straightening everything out? She had no idea how long she had been unconscious and it was impossible to tell what time of day or night it was in the room.

The door opened and the female agent came in. She had light blonde hair worn high in a tight bun that seemed to pull at her scalp. She had bright blue eyes that were cold, calculating. She sat down across from Cindy and looked her over as though trying to make up her mind about something.

She leaned back in her chair, before speaking. "So, are you ready to talk?"

"I don't know what's happening. This is just some terrible mistake," Cindy blurted out. "Did you call Detective Walters?"

"He's been contacted. He was very interested to see the file we've been building on you," the woman said.

"I don't understand what's going on," Cindy pleaded.

"I'll tell you what's going on. We've been tracking Heinrich for several months now, ever since he contacted an art dealer in regard to a certain valuable painting that went missing during World War II. We were waiting to close in on him because although we knew where he was, we didn't know the location where he'd stashed the majority of the artwork in his possession. We also knew he had an accomplice, but we didn't know who. We were waiting to pick him up until we could ascertain those two things. He was clever, though, always careful except for the one slip up with Haverston.

"Then he got himself killed and you came out of the woodwork. Very clever of you, by the way, pretending to find that one piece of art in his house. Convenient that it was later stolen. Only his accomplice could have suspected that what appeared to be a worthless piece of art was far from it."

"Please, I don't know this man. I never even met him. Detective Walters had my friend Jeremiah translating the Hebrew writings in the house and I took him over dinner. I found the painting by accident. Jeremiah can tell you."

"Oh, I assure you, he's being questioned closely about your involvement in this entire situation."

"They both know me," Cindy said. "They'll both vouch for me."

"They might be willing to vouch for you, but how well does either of them really know you?" the woman asked, arching a brow.

"Really well!"

"Is that a fact? I think they'd be surprised to learn that your father's engineering firm did work several years ago in Germany."

"What? No, I don't think Dad was ever in Germany," Cindy said, struggling to think. "But, I don't know, all I knew was he was gone a lot. What does that even matter where my dad was?"

"Maybe your friends would also be surprised to learn that your brother, Kyle, took a little trip to Germany in between filming seasons of his television show and did a little excavation of abandoned mines. You know, the kinds of places that looted art treasures were hidden in by Nazis?"

"When did Kyle do that?" Cindy whispered.

The truth was, it could have happened at any time. She had made a point of not following her brother's career and her mom never talked about what Kyle did that wasn't newsworthy in the read-about-your-brother-in-a-magazine kind of way. The truth was, she had no idea what he did in his private life.

"And maybe they'd be fascinated to know that the first place you rented in this area, the one on Goose Creek Road, was owned by Heinrich Beck."

Cindy couldn't help but stare. She felt like she was going to be sick. "I dealt with a property manager. I didn't know who the owner was. I wasn't even there long before I started renting from a guy who rented his house to staff members of the church. This is just a bunch of coincidences."

The woman slammed her fist down on the table, making Cindy jump. "We might not be able to prove your family's involvement with Beck, but we can prove yours."

She snapped her fingers and the door opened and Agent Davies came in with a folder. He sat down and pulled out several photos. He pushed the first one across the table toward Cindy. "You and Beck three weeks ago."

Cindy stared at the picture. It was her sitting on a bench in the park where Jeremiah liked to take Captain to run. Three weeks ago she had gone with them and played some fetch with Captain. She had sat down on a bench for a couple of minutes while Jeremiah took a turn. There, sitting on the same bench as she was, was an old man. He had his lips parted and it almost looked like he was talking.

She racked her brain, trying to remember. She remembered going to the park and she remembered sitting down on the bench. After a moment she remembered the old man as well.

"That's Heinrich?" she asked. She hadn't seen his body.

"As if you didn't know," the woman sneered.

"What did he say to you?"

It came back to Cindy in a rush. "He was watching Jeremiah play with his dog. And he said 'he seems like a good man.' I wasn't sure if he was actually talking to me or even talking about Jeremiah. I said, 'yes, he is,' in case he was. That was it. He got up and left."

"And what exactly is your explanation for this picture?" Davies asked, sliding another picture across the cold metal table toward her.

Cindy picked it up, her handcuffs clinking together as she did and stared at it. She was walking into her house in the background and there, in the foreground, parked in a car on her street and staring at her was Heinrich.

"That was taken five days ago."

Her head began to spin. "I don't understand," she whispered.

He began to slide more pictures across the table, all of them showing her and somewhere in it Heinrich.

"He was following me? Why?" she asked.

"These were all taken over the course of the last three months," the woman said. "We've been watching him for months, but it's only recently that he got so sloppy when it came to his meetings with you."

"This isn't true. I wasn't meeting with him. I don't know him. I don't know anything, especially why he was stalking me."

She felt like her mind was shattering, scattering into tiny fragments and flying apart. The world was upside down. Three months. That was how long ago he had met briefly with Jeremiah. Did she dare mention that or would they just think that Jeremiah was a conspirator, too?

She couldn't think and her chest was tightening up so it felt like she couldn't breathe. She could hear herself taking short, gasping breaths and in a part of her brain that was still functioning she was wondering if she was hyperventilating.

"I...want...a...lawyer," she finally managed to gasp.

This wasn't just a misunderstanding. These people truly believed that she was guilty of the things they were saying. What if Mark couldn't convince them otherwise? She had been arrested, the full force of that hit her. What would people think? What would happen if she went to court? Surely they couldn't prove all of this, not enough to convince a jury.

I can't go to jail, she thought. As the thought came to her it seemed like the walls of the room that she was in were closing in on her. She thought about the endless days she had spent trapped, confined, imprisoned after being kidnapped in Hawaii. Jail would be worse. There would be no hope of rescue, and possible torture at the hands of guards and other inmates.

"You'll see a lawyer when we're done talking," the woman said.

And that wasn't right. Cindy closed her fist around the photograph she was still holding and jumped to her feet. She was about to do something, she didn't know what, when the door flew open. A tall man stood in shadow. "That's enough for now," he said.

The two agents stood up. Davies scooped up the photos, tucked them in his folder, and they left the room. The door slammed shut behind them and Cindy sank down into her chair. She opened her fist and stared at the crinkled up photograph that she had been holding when she started to lose it.

She wanted to remember that day and figure out why Heinrich had been there, watching her. That might be the only thing that could save her now.

Mark was heading home when he decided to drop into the precinct and grab the jacket he'd left there earlier that morning with the coffee stain on it. Traci would be running errands the next day and that would include dropping by the drycleaners.

His plan was to get in, get the jacket, and get out. He was exhausted and he wanted nothing more at this point than a hot meal and some time vegging on the couch. He made it to his desk, grabbed the jacket, and glanced down. There were a couple of messages that had been scrawled out for him.

"Leave it until the morning," he breathed, even as he realized he was reaching to pick them up.

There were three. The first two could definitely wait for the morning. The third one caused him to pause.

Dave W. called about Cindy and the FBI.

Nothing in that sentence made any sense. There was a local number. He would have dropped it back on his desk but for the mention of Cindy. Nothing that ever happened with the secretary was delay worthy.

He pulled out his phone just in time to see that the battery was dying. He picked up his desk phone instead and called the number.

"Hello?" a male voice answered.

"Hi, I'm looking for a Dave W."

"That's me, Dave Wyman."

"Wildman! This is Detective Mark Walters. I got a very cryptic message from you."

"Detective! Why did the F.B.I. arrest Cindy?"

"What? I'm sorry, you said, what?"

"Two agents came by the church and arrested Cindy almost two hours ago. They dragged her out of here in handcuffs."

Mark sat down at his desk. "I have no idea what you're talking about. Do you know the names of the agents?"

"The man was named Davies and I have no idea what the woman's name was. I didn't even get close to them. I just heard Cindy screaming for help, for someone to call you. By the time I ran out of my office and got to the parking lot they were gone."

"Thank you for calling. I'm going to go deal with this," Mark said.

He hung up and sat for a moment, stunned. There weren't even words to express what he was thinking. Finally he shook himself into action. This was all ridiculous, the world's worst misunderstanding, but given how fragile Cindy was at the moment, the timing could not have possibly been worse.

He called his friend at the Bureau who picked up on the second ring.

"It's Mark."

"Hey, Mark, twice in one day, I'm a bit surprised."

"Vince, what in the he- what's going on over there?"

"What do you mean?"

"I just heard that two hours ago an agent named Davies and his partner arrested Cindy Preston, the church secretary. I want to know how that screw up happened and it needs to be resolved now."

"Slow down there, now what did you say has happened?"

Mark repeated himself.

"Okay, let me get back to you, I need to check and see what's going on."

"You do that," Mark spit out. "And call me back at this number."

The call ended and Mark sat, just staring at his phone, willing it to ring. This whole situation was not only inconceivable, but it was also intolerable. As the minutes ticked slowly by he decided that calling in the

Feds had been the biggest mistake he could have made, regardless of the scope of the case and the international entanglements and implications.

The phone rang and he jumped. "Hello?"

"Hi, Mark?"

"Yes."

"This is Cindy's roommate, Geanie. I tried your cell first and then Cindy has this number listed below. I know this is probably going to sound strange, but she didn't come home from work and I know she's not with Jeremiah, and given everything-"

"I can't explain right now, but she's going to be okay. I'll tell you more when I can," he said.

"Oh, thank you."

"Uh huh."

He hung up, took a deep breath, and called Traci to explain why he was going to be later than he'd thought. She was even more outraged than he was and told him that he shouldn't come home until Cindy was safe. Then she offered to bring dinner to him. As he hung up he acknowledged again to himself that he had the greatest wife in the world.

When she showed up half an hour later with steak and roasted potatoes he was practically climbing the walls. He had just tried calling his friend again and had left a message when he didn't answer.

"No word?" Traci said, looking supremely worried, as she set two plates down on his desk.

He shook his head.

She reached out and squeezed his arm. "It will be okay. You'll get this all sorted out."

"Hey, Mrs. Walters," an officer said as he walked by.

"Hello."

"Mrs. Walters!" another called from across the room.

She waved back.

It went on that way until nearly every officer had gone out of his way to greet her. It was a strange thing. As much as they all shunned him, they all universally embraced her. He wasn't sure if it was because they knew that she had stood by him and been true blue or if it was because they knew that she had been the one to talk him out of killing the suspect he had tortured and had gotten him to leave the interrogation room. Whatever it was, she was adored by all.

She sat down and they began to eat dinner. It wasn't how he had wanted to spend an evening with her, but it beat sitting and waiting by himself. Her very presence had a calming effect on him. He figured it must have always been that way, but it's something that he had taken special note of ever since the incident.

"It will be okay," she said again when they were halfway through their meal.

He wasn't sure if she was saying it for her own benefit or for his, but he was grateful either way.

"It's just so crazy," he said.

"I know, and they'll see that and it will all be straightened out. She should make them crawl giving her an apology, though," Traci noted.

Mark smiled at that. "Cindy's not the type."

"It would do her good to be a little more assertive every once in a while," Traci noted.

"I'm sure you could help her work on that," Mark said.

She nodded resolutely.

It all felt surreal, but as he kept reminding himself, there really was nothing more he could do than wait. Storming down to the nearest Fed building would do nobody any good. In fact, it might just get him arrested, especially if he made the kind of threats he was in the mood to make.

He took a deep breath. Jeremiah would be at the synagogue doing his rabbi thing. That was probably a blessing. By the time he found out about this it would all be over. He didn't need him going all loose cannon either.

As if she'd read his mind Traci suddenly asked, "What is the deal with Cindy and Jeremiah anyway?"

He actually laughed out loud. "Darling, that is the million dollar question as it turns out. If you figure it out, make sure to tell me."

"Ditto," she said with a smile.

His phone rang and he snatched it up, dropping steak in his lap as he did so. "Hello?"

"Mark, it's Vince."

"Well, what's going on?"

"I've just been talking to the agents assigned to the case. They've spent most of the day going over what you sent them. They both agree that Cindy is in no way a suspect."

"That's good news."

"Not the good news you're hoping for. Mark, what I'm trying to say is, we didn't arrest Cindy."

"What? But Agent Davies-"

"That's just it. We don't have an Agent Davies working here. We have no idea who grabbed her."

Mark turned to Traci who was staring at him, eager to hear the news. "It's all happening again," he whispered.

"What?" she asked.

He felt the receiver slip from his fingers and he heard it hit the desk. This wasn't happening. There was no way he could call the rabbi and tell him.

Traci reached over and snatched up the receiver. "Hello? This is Mark's wife, Traci. What's happened?"

He heard her scream as if it was coming from somewhere far away. He couldn't live through this again. He stood up. He had to go. He had to do...something...if only he could remember what it was.

Everyone in the precinct had stopped when they heard Traci scream and they were facing them, staring, wondering what was happening. Then he felt Traci's hand gripping his shoulder, putting a tremendous amount of pressure downward on it. It got his attention and he turned to look at her.

She was climbing onto his desk with a look on her face he had never seen before. What was she doing. She stood up in the middle of his desk and shouted. "Listen up, people!"

She already had their attention but her shout had the effect of making everyone freeze in place, as though transfixed by the sound of her voice. Everyone was staring up at her. "We've just had word from the F.B.I. that a man and a woman masquerading as agents kidnapped Cindy Preston from First Shepherd Church earlier this evening. That's right, I said Cindy Preston.

You all know the name and with good cause. She's just a church secretary but she's done more for this precinct and the people of this community in the last two years than most people could hope to accomplish in an entire lifetime. Now she's in trouble and only we can save her. I need every man here working on this case and nothing else until it's solved and she's been found!"

Mark stared, stunned. Traci had no official connection to the police department. She couldn't make such demands. But there she stood, fierce, determined, glorious in her certainty that this would be solved. He glanced around the room and he realized that the respect the other officers held her in had been transformed in a moment to awe.

He wanted to say something, to stop her, but he was powerless. She had become a force of nature. He turned and saw his captain standing outside his office, arms folded across his chest, a stern look on his face and he cringed inside. The man hadn't wanted him back on the force, he'd made that very clear. This was just the excuse he needed to get rid of Mark permanently. And then there'd be nothing he could ever do to help Cindy again.

Silence fell as Traci stopped speaking. You could have heard a pin drop. And then, from his position next to his office, the captain boomed, "You heard the lady, everyone move, now, now, now!"

The room exploded into a flurry of action. Officers were heading for the doors, others were picking up phones and calling in those who were at home. Mark just stood, dumbfounded.

"Walters, get in here!" the captain barked, jerking his thumb toward his office.

"Yes, sir," Traci said, as she climbed down off the desk.

"Not you," he said, his face softening slightly. "Send your husband in."

Traci put a hand on the small of his back and shoved. Mark stumbled forward. He was going to face his doom, but at least there would be others to try and find Cindy.

He made it into the office and slumped into his chair. The captain leaned against his desk.

"Give me one good reason why I shouldn't fire you and hire your wife," he snarled.

"I was smart enough to marry her," Mark said.

"Okay, fair enough."

"Listen. We all owe Cindy and most of us heard what happened to her over there in Hawaii. I've looked over the files and this entire case is the biggest mess I've ever seen in my thirty years on the force. It stinks to high heaven and nobody's going to come out of this smelling good. The Feds are going to do whatever they're going to do at this point. The three dead people, the art, all that crap, leave it to them. The only thing I want you to do is find the secretary and get her back because she's going to be the last thing they're thinking about at this point.

"I know you know how to get things done when you set your mind to it," the captain said ominously. "Don't be shy. Grab somebody, whoever will partner up with you on this, and go get it done. I don't want to see your face back in this office until she's home safe. You got me?"

"I got you," Mark said, standing up and heading to the door. He felt like he was walking in a dream. He couldn't believe his captain had been implying what he thought he had been. Still, he wasn't about to question him, not at this point. He walked to his desk, picked up the phone and called Liam.

"Get down here as fast as you possibly can and prepare to be out until the job's done."

"What's the job?"

"I'll fill you in later. And Liam, bring your guns?"

Liam paused. "My service weapon?"

"How many other guns you got?"

"Quite a few. My grandfather was a collector."

"Bring them all."

He slammed the phone down, turned and spied an officer in the crowd. "Daniels!"

The officer in question turned, startled. "Detective?"

"You're a hacker, right?"

"I'm good with computers, but I'm not-"

"Cut the crap. I don't have time for it. Are you or are you not?"

Daniels turned beet red. "Are."

"Good, get over here, you're with me."

"What should I do?" Traci asked, breathlessly.

He put his hands on her shoulders and looked her in the eyes. "I've got a really important job for you."

"What?"

"I need you to go tell Jeremiah what's happened. You're the only messenger I can send that I don't think he'll kill."

"I'm on it," she said with a nod. She grabbed the back of his head, kissed him hard, and then spun on her heel and headed for the front door.

"Yup," Mark said. "Smart enough to marry her."

"What is it you're going to need me to do?" Daniels asked.

Mark turned. "You're the best computer guy in the office, and I've heard rumors about some of the things you do on your own time."

"I don't do anything illeg-"

"I don't care," Mark interrupted him. "I need you to track a vehicle that left the First Shepherd parking lot at approximately 4:50 p.m. There are traffic cams at the intersections closest to that church. Can you do that?"

Daniels grimaced. "I've been telling the captain for two years that if we got the Ghostrider software and some equipment we could track vehicles no problem like they can in some of the bigger cities."

"Yeah, time to prove that you can do that without the fancy software."

"Traffic cams, sure, but if we need to pull from parking lot security cameras and ATMs we need to talk to the banks and the stores and get permission and access to their feeds."

Mark stepped close so that his nose was inches from Daniels. "No. We. Don't."

Daniels stared at him for a moment.

"Understood?"

"Understood," Daniels said before dropping his eyes and turning away. "Let me get to my computer."

The larger stores, the chains, and banks had their security feeds networked instead of on a closed circuit.

Mark knew that someone with the right skills could access that information without him having to track down branch and store managers after hours and save them a lot of time.

In his gut he knew that they didn't have time to waste.

Jeremiah was grateful for once that it was a light service that evening. Few people at his synagogue attended the night that Rosh Hashanah started, instead spending that time with family or alone in reflection. The services the next two days would be much more packed. He was going to have to give in when he got home tonight and take some of the stronger pain killers so he could get enough sleep to be prepared.

He was dead on his feet and the pain was gnawing at him. It didn't help that he was taking pains to hide the fact that he was injured. His congregation worried enough as it was without giving them more reason to. Thanks to Marie he already had a second mother, he didn't need a hundred more.

"It is our duty to praise the Master of all, to ascribe greatness to the Molder of primeval creation ... Therefore, we put our hope in you, L-rd our G-d, that we may soon see Your mighty splendor... On that day, the L-rd will be One and His Name will be One," he said, reciting the Aleinu prayer used to close out most services.

He took a deep breath. "L'shanah tovah," he said.

"L'shanah tovah," those in attendance responded.

As everyone began to leave he was grateful that no one seemed intent on lingering and mingling. It was a good sign that they were focused and reflecting as they should be. It was an even better sign that he might be able to get home shortly.

He'd promised Cindy that he would call for a ride home. As he headed for his office he called her. The phone rang several times and then went to voicemail. He left a message. He was about to try her home when a shadow crossed his path.

He looked up quickly. A woman was walking toward him, the light from the building nearest the parking lot shining behind her. He squinted, wondering for a moment if it was Cindy and if she had been waiting for him. If he'd known he would have invited her to sit in the service.

A moment later, though, he realized it wasn't her. He recognized Traci, Mark's wife. He didn't need to see her face to realize that something was dreadfully wrong. They barely knew each other and he couldn't fathom what would have caused her to drive to see him in person when she could have called. It wasn't like her husband didn't have his number. Unless, something had happened to him.

"What's happened?" he asked as she came to a stop in front of him. "Is Mark okay?"

"Not really, but he's not the problem," she said.

"I don't understand. If something didn't happen to him, then why are you here?"

She reached out and put a hand on his good arm. "I've come to tell you that Cindy has been taken."

"That's not funny," he said.

"It's not meant to be."

"She was taken from the church by two people pretending to be F.B.I. agents. We have every man on the force working on finding her as we speak."

"Taken from the church?" Jeremiah repeated. "When?"

"A few minutes before five."

"How long has Mark known?" Jeremiah asked, feeling a deadly cold settle into the pit of his stomach.

"That she wasn't being held by the F.B.I.? About twenty minutes. He sent me here to tell you while he works on finding her."

Jeremiah balled his hands into fists. Mark was more clever than he realized. He had sent the one person he was sure Jeremiah wouldn't hurt to deliver the news. "He should have told me the moment he knew something had happened to her."

"I don't disagree," Traci said, "but what's done is done. There's nothing we can do now but wait."

"I beg to differ," he said.

He turned and sprinted toward the parking lot.

He heard a startled cry and then the sound of high heels chasing after him. He made it to the parking lot, vaulted the hedge separating the synagogue parking lot from the church parking lot, and barreled onto church grounds. His mind registered that the gate was already open.

Moments later the church office came into sight. The door was open, lights blazed from the windows, and he could see police officers just inside the door. He slowed to a halt. They would have already contaminated the crime scene.

Traci ran up beside him and he was surprised at how quickly she'd made it. "You see, I told you, every officer on the force is working to find her," she said.

He ground his teeth.

A familiar figure walked out of the office and Jeremiah made a beeline for him.

Dave turned. "Jeremiah," he said, "what are you doing here?"

"Same thing they are. Tell me what happened."

"I was in my office, getting ready to go home for the night when I heard screaming outside. It sounded like Cindy. I ran out of the building, but couldn't see her. All I saw was Roy, the head pastor, standing in the door to the office. I thought for a moment she was in there, but then I realized she couldn't be. I heard her shouting for someone to help, to call the detective or you. It sounded like she was in the parking lot. By the time I got out here, she and whoever took her were gone. I called Mark and left a message. I tried calling the synagogue, but I just got the answering machine. I didn't see your car and I didn't know your home number. When Mark called me back I told him what had happened. Then he called me a few minutes ago and asked me to open up the church for officers."

"So, you didn't see who took her?"

Dave shook his head. "No. Roy said the F.B.I. had arrested her, but that made no sense. He saw what they looked like."

"Is he here now?"

"No, but I told Mark he should call him for a description. He told me it was a man and a woman who took Cindy."

"Why didn't he help her?" Jeremiah demanded.

"I don't know. He seemed to think that if they were arresting her, she must have done something to deserve it. I couldn't quite believe it."

"Is he insane?" Jeremiah asked.

Dave winced. "No, but he tends to be more a man of judgment than mercy, especially in times of stress."

"I'm going to need you to give me his home address and forget that you did so," Jeremiah said.

Dave licked his lips and nodded. "He lives over on Walnut. The green house at the end of the cul-de-sac."

"Thank you," Jeremiah said before spinning on his heel.

Traci was there, right in front of him. Her face was white and strained. "What are you going to do?" she asked.

"That's none of your concern," he said, unable to check the coldness in his voice.

"I saw Mark like this once, it didn't end well," she told him.

Jeremiah permitted himself a small smile. "Believe me when I tell you. I am nothing like your husband."

She fell away from him with a small gasp and he walked past. The coldness in his stomach was settling over his entire body. It was an old, familiar feeling and he welcomed it because he knew it brought with it the strength to do whatever he must no matter the cost.

He had lied to Cindy in his delirium hours before. He had told her he had once been a different man. As he walked to the parking lot, though, he knew that wasn't true. He was still the same man he always had been. He was just better at hiding it. That was okay because he knew what he had to do.

He made it to Cindy's car. He knew that her purse was probably still inside the office, but he didn't have time to try and get it or her keys away from them. He walked up to her car, broke the window, hotwired it, and thirty seconds later was driving out of the lot.

It would probably take them forever to realize the car was even missing. And by then he'd have done what he needed to.

He didn't bother driving home. He drove straight to Pastor Roy's house. He'd met the man only a couple of times and he'd never liked him. Not that that made this easier. It was already easy. He stood in the way of information he needed about Cindy's captors.

Jeremiah parked out front and as he walked up to the front door debated whether he'd even bother knocking or just break straight in. In the end he decided to knock so that Roy wouldn't have even a moment to try and call 911 before he could get his hands on him.

He rang the doorbell, knowing that if he pounded on the door that, too, might raise the man's suspicions. A few seconds later he could tell that someone was standing on the other side of the door, probably looking out the peephole. Jeremiah forced a smile onto his face.

The door opened and Roy stood there, a look of surprise on his face.

"Rabbi? What brings you here?"

"A matter of grave concern to both of us. Do you mind if I come in so we can talk?"

"No, not at all," Roy said. His body language was closed off, already hostile. He wasn't open to anything

Jeremiah might have to say on any topic. That was just fine by him.

He stepped inside the hallway and glanced around. It was a nice house, nothing fancy. There was a picture on the wall of Roy and a woman with gray hair. They were both smiling.

"I didn't know you were married," Jeremiah said.

Roy glanced in the direction he was looking. "My wife passed away a few years ago. It's just me now."

Jeremiah nodded. He had already guessed that since there were no other photos of children or grandchildren immediately visible but there were a few other pictures that looked like they were of his wife. He had loved her. On some level it was nice to know that he had been capable of caring about somebody other than himself.

"I'm sorry to hear that she's passed away."

Roy closed the door. He locked it and then turned to look at Jeremiah. "Well, it comforts me to know that one day I'll go and join her," he said, trying to sound optimistic.

Jeremiah turned, and quick as lightning wrapped his right hand around the man's throat and slammed him against the wall. The pastor gasped and clawed at his hand, which just made Jeremiah tighten his grip.

"That day is going to be today unless you tell me everything I need to know about the people who kidnapped Cindy."

Mark's phone rang and he snatched it up. "Walters."

"I think Jeremiah's going to do something he shouldn't," Traci said.

Mark closed his eyes. "I was afraid of that. He didn't hurt you or anything did he?"

"No."

"Then that's the only miracle I think we're entitled to in that direction. I can't worry about him right now. Can you get home, lock the door? Or better yet, can you go over to a friend's house? These guys have been one step ahead of us from the start and I don't want to have to worry about them grabbing you."

"Yes. I can go stay with my folks. They've been wanting to talk to me about my sister and I've been putting it off."

"Great, go. That way I'll know you're safe."

"Just as long as you promise to be safe," she countered.

"I will do everything in my power," he said.

"I love you."

"Not half as much as I love you. Call me when you get there."

She hung up and as Mark put the receiver back in its cradle he saw Liam coming toward him and from the looks of it he had taken Mark seriously. He was loaded for bear.

"I've never seen so many weapons on one person before," Mark admitted as Liam stopped at his desk.

"The rest are in the car."

"Some of those aren't even legal to own."

Liam shrugged. "I inherited them from my grandpa. I told you. He was a collector."

That might be so, but Liam hadn't surrendered those particular weapons when he'd inherited them. Mark felt himself starting to smile. Before he could say anything, Daniels got up from his computer station and hurried over.

"Well?" Mark asked.

"I was able to track the van to a warehouse district and then I lost it. It's probably somewhere right in that area."

"Let's go then, you're coming with us," Mark said.

Outside Mark got into his car and plugged his phone in to start charging. Daniels got in the front seat while Liam and all his gear ended up in the back.

A minute later they were on the road with Daniels directing.

"There's only a couple of warehouses that are shut down. If they stayed in the area without changing cars and leaving then they're likely to be in one of them. I doubt one of the manufacturing companies has them on the payroll and it would be harder for them to find a quiet corner to hide out."

Twenty minutes later they were on the outskirts of town in the warehouse district. It wasn't a large area. Most of the manufacturing in the area was located closer to Los Angeles, but there was still about a dozen warehouses. Some were used for construction and others for storage. Daniels had already checked and knew that four were supposed to be empty, belonging to businesses that had gone belly-up sometime in the past few years.

They pulled up across the street from the first one. Everything was dark, but then he had expected that it would be. It was unlikely that the people they were looking for would advertise their presence.

The three of them got out of the car and headed toward the front of the building. There was an office door next to a loading dock and they made for that. Mark didn't see any cars in the vicinity but that also didn't mean anything.

They had just reached the door when he heard a dog bark. He spun and saw a figure coming around the corner carrying a flashlight, a dog at his side.

"Police!" Mark called, tensing, prepared to give chase or find cover depending on what the figure did.

Instead the man picked up speed, walking straight for them, the flashlight bouncing around like crazy. When the man and dog were closer he saw that the dog was a Labrador mix. He couldn't make out the man's features, though, because he was shining the flashlight full on them.

Liam moved to the side, out of the shaft of light, effectively flanking the newcomer.

Smart move, Mark thought.

"Detective, is that you? I haven't seen you since Thanksgiving! Rascal, you remember the man?"

Mark squinted, trying to make out the features of the man holding the flashlight.

"It's me, Harry! I was supposed to be at the Thanksgiving party at Cindy's that you busted up, but I was in the hospital."

The guard lowered the flashlight and Mark saw an older man with short cropped gray hair and a weathered face. He stared in shock as he realized that it was indeed Harry, one of the homeless men that had participated in the big charity event from the year before pairing the homeless with dogs to care for. Had he not identified himself Mark would never have recognized him. He had cleaned up considerably from what he remembered.

He dropped his eyes to the dog. "I see the two of you are doing well. What exactly is it that you're doing here?"

"Security guard!" Harry said, puffing out his chest with pride. "Bank hired me and Rascal a few months back to patrol the place. Seems people were constantly breaking into the building, trashing it, you know. We run 'em off. It's a good job. Decent pay."

"So, you're not living on the streets anymore?"

"Nope. Rascal and I got a little flat. It's not much, but it keeps the rain off and it's got both air conditioning and heating."

"That's great," he said. He gathered himself. "Have you seen Cindy?"

"Not for a few months. I used to see her dropping stuff off at the shelter every once in a while. Been meaning to let her know about my new habitation, but just haven't gotten around to it. If you could tell her, I'd appreciate it."

Mark shook his head. "No, I mean, tonight."

"Tonight? What would she be doing around here?"

"She's been kidnapped. A man and a woman dressed like Feds grabbed her and we think they brought her to this area in a black van."

"Who would do something like that?" Harry said, his face flushing with anger.

"Bad people. Have you seen anything?"

"No, my building's locked up tight. Wait, you said a black van?"

"Yes."

"I saw one just as we were getting here today. It was heading that way," Harry said, pointing down the street. "I didn't see where it went, though. You need any help looking?"

"No, we've got this. But keep your eyes out. You got a phone?"

"Sure. Company gave it to me," Harry said.

Mark pulled a card out of his pocket. "Here's my number, call if you see anything," Mark said.

"Will do. And you get her back safe. She's a nice lady."

"We'll try, Harry."

Mark turned and headed back to the car.

"The direction he pointed leads to the old bakery," Daniels said. "That's the only empty building down that way.

"At least that narrows it down slightly."

They drove without headlights on and parked a hundred yards from the building in question. "Okay, everyone ready?" Mark asked. "We're going in fast and quiet. Remember, be sure of your targets. We don't want to risk hitting Cindy."

Both Liam and Daniels nodded.

Roy was terrified. Jeremiah could smell the stench of fear all over him. But he had given him the descriptions he was looking for of the man and woman who took Cindy.

Still, he held him, pinned to the wall, his hand around his throat. He knew just how much to squeeze, just how much pressure to apply to cause panic but no bruising. It was a delicate balance, and the amount of effort it was taking him to restrain himself was herculean.

"Thank you for your cooperation," he spat at him.

"This, this is assault," Roy said. The man was too stupid to keep his mouth shut and pray for deliverance. In another time, in another place, it would have cost him his life.

"Technically, it's battery. If you're going to accuse someone of something, get your facts straight first," Jeremiah hissed. He let go of Roy's throat and took a step back. "Like Cindy, by your silence, your lack of action, you as much as accused her of being a criminal when nothing could be farther from the truth."

"How was I supposed to know those people weren't F.B.I.?"

"You could have checked their identification. As her boss you could have, should have demanded more of an explanation. You should have at the very least been suspicious that no one was questioning you or your staff about her recent activities."

"I'll be pressing charges against you," he blustered.

"Not if you're smart, you won't. After all, it's just your word against mine and I was very careful not to leave a mark on you. Besides, you're going to be too busy defending yourself."

"Against what?" the man asked, his chin quivering slightly.

"Oh, you have a lot to answer for, and trust me, I'll make sure that they prosecute you to the fullest extent of the law."

"I've done nothing illegal! There's nothing they could charge me with," Roy protested.

"How about accessory after the fact for failure to report a kidnapping? Or possibly obstruction of justice for not providing police officers with descriptions of the kidnappers? I mean, after all, it's been how long since you learned that it absolutely was a kidnapping and you haven't called the police to tell them what you know, or even gone down to the church where they're at right now desperately searching for evidence?" Jeremiah shook his head. "What makes me sick is that you call yourself a pastor. You should have looked out for your flock, you should have been the first to Cindy's defense as her boss and her spiritual leader. And you should be down there right now doing everything in your power to help her. Your secretary has been kidnapped and yet you do nothing. You're not just a bad person. You're a bad pastor."

Jeremiah turned and stalked out the door. He dearly wanted to snap the man's neck instead, but the scum wasn't worth it.

He got back into Cindy's car and drove off. The descriptions Roy had given meant nothing to him. Hopefully, Mark would recognize them.

He dialed the detective who answered in hushed tones.

"I have a description of the kidnappers."

"We think we found where they're holding her. I'll call you back when I know more."

Jeremiah hoped Mark was right and that in a few minutes he'd be talking to Cindy himself. On the off chance that wasn't the case, he had a couple more leads he could follow.

He fished a card out his pocket, dialed the number on it, and a moment later a man's voice with a thick German accent answered.

Cindy felt like she'd been staring at the crinkled picture of Heinrich in his car outside her house for an hour. Her eyes were beginning to hurt and she forced herself to close them for a minute. The F.B.I. agents hadn't come back yet which made her suspicious.

Actually, the more she thought about it, the more suspicious she became of everything. She had no idea how the agency actually functioned, but she would have thought they would have allowed her a phone call, let her contact an attorney, or even read her her rights. Then again, maybe it was only police that had to make those concessions. She really didn't know.

She got up and inspected the room. There was no one way mirror or anything like that so she would think there had to be some kind of surveillance camera documenting what was happening inside the room. She looked around for one, but couldn't find it. That didn't mean there wasn't one, but it was one more thing that just seemed off somehow.

She wondered what she would find if she was able to walk out the door. She had regained consciousness in this room so she hadn't even seen the building or anyone else but the two agents and the man who had interrupted them. She could be in a federal office building or in some warehouse somewhere for all she knew.

Maybe it was because the whole experience was causing her to have flashbacks to being kidnapped, but she was starting to seriously wonder if the people who had her really were agents. She struggled to remember what the badge Davies had flashed at her looked like. She remembered seeing it for just a moment and it had been just a badge, no identification card or anything.

She sat down and glanced again at the photo. It was proof that he had been watching her, not that they had been meeting or interacting. If the F.B.I. had really been watching Heinrich for weeks as they claimed wouldn't they have made their presence known much sooner, like as soon as he turned up dead? Or they should have at least reached out to local law enforcement which would have been Mark since he was the lead detective on the case.

When they discovered the piece of the Amber Room they should have been right there to confiscate it. If they'd really been doing this much surveillance they couldn't have helped but notice that officers spent a huge chunk of time removing pieces of it from the house.

Whoever they were they clearly had been following Heinrich, and he had clearly been following her. They couldn't be from the bureau, though. They were willing to pretend they were, though, to find out what she might know. And the fact that they thought she knew anything told her that in some ways she knew more than they did.

One thing was clear. Regardless of who these people really were, she needed a chance to escape or at least reach a phone so she could tell Mark what was going on. She didn't know how long she had been there, but if someone at the church had heard her shouting and actually called him, he should have already been talking to the F.B.I.. In fact, the fact that she was still here without having heard from him in some way, even having him be ushered into the room to tell her there was nothing he could do for her, felt like more proof that whoever these people were they weren't government.

At least, not her government. It was possible that they were attached to the German or Russian consulates or whoever else it was that was looking for the lost art treasures. For all she knew one of them was the one who had shot Jeremiah.

She lowered her head onto the desk in a seeming act of defeat in case there was a camera in the room watching. They had used her father's job and a supposed trip by her brother to try and bully her. She had no idea if either of them had even been in Germany. Two could play that game.

A minute later she heard the door open and she felt a thrill of triumph. They were watching her and she was right that putting her head down would get their attention. She heard a chair move and someone sat down across from her.

She counted to ten in her head before slowly looking up, making sure to move as though she was exhausted.

The blonde woman was sitting across from her, staring at her like a vulture watching a dying animal.

"I'll tell you what you want to know about Great Uncle Heinrich," Cindy said.

The woman blinked rapidly and Cindy knew the response had caught her by surprise. "At least you're finally acknowledging that he's your uncle," the woman said at last.

Cindy nodded. "I didn't know he'd involved my father and my brother. I thought I was the only one in the family he'd reached out to. But, I mean, why bother hiding it? You guys already know everything anyway."

"Yes, we do," the woman said in very careful tones. She folded her hands on top of the table. "Except, of course, for the most important thing."

"Where he's hidden the art?" Cindy asked.

The woman nodded and there was an intense gleam in her eye. She looked like she was practically going to start salivating.

"I'll take you to them, but only if I can get some kind of deal, you know, for cooperating."

"Tell us where to find them and I'm sure we could work something out."

"I can't tell you where they are. He only took me once, but I can retrace the route. So, I'll take you there, but first you have to agree to give me immunity."

The woman looked like she was on the verge of just saying yes, but she forced herself under control and stood. "Give me a minute to see what I can do."

"Okay," Cindy said, before letting her head sink slowly back down on the table.

She had already decided where she was going to lead them. Now she needed to figure out a way to leave a sign in case Mark found this place by some miracle. She would have given anything for a pen or pencil.

Then she thought about the walls Heinrich had covered in writing, including the last thing he had ever written.

She took her index finger on her left hand and dug it into the index finger of her right hand as hard as she could, scratching through the skin until blood bubbled to the surface. Then, squeezing the finger to keep the blood flowing, she began to write on the edge of the table in very tiny letters, keeping her head down to hide exactly what it was she was doing.

Five minutes passed. Cindy had finished writing her word on the table and was waiting, tense, ready for one of her captors to return. She forced herself to take deep, even breaths. She had to remain calm, focused, or everything would be lost.

Suddenly she heard raised voices just outside. She lifted her head just as the door flew open with a crash.

17

Cindy stared at the blonde woman standing there. Something had changed. She was much more tense. "We have to go now," the woman said.

The fact that they were moving her was good. There would be a greater opportunity to try and escape. She couldn't seem too eager, though, or it might be suspicious.

"What about my immunity?" Cindy asked, remembering to stay in character.

The woman rushed forward and grabbed Cindy by the arm, hauling her to her feet. "You can have it if you can take us there right now."

"Okay, why the rush?" She stopped short of asking if she could have the deal in writing. She wanted to be believable, not throw up obstacles to getting out of there.

The woman blinked at her, clearly struggling for a believable lie. "We've just had a source inform us that the Germans are closing in on the location of your uncle's stash. We mustn't let them reach it and steal the artwork."

Cindy nodded, and let the woman drag her out the door. All she saw was a dim hallway before the woman shoved her out another door into a dark alleyway where a car was waiting. She was pushed into the backseat and the door was slammed behind her.

Davies was behind the wheel and the woman jumped in the passenger seat. A moment later they were speeding away from wherever they had been. It looked like an alley of some sort, but Cindy had no idea where in the city they might be, or even if they still were in the city since she didn't know how long they'd driven to get here.

She smelled burning rubber as Davies took a hard turn and shot out onto a road. Her hands were still cuffed in front of her, but she was alone in the backseat.

She wondered if she could open the door, jump, and escape that way.

She looked out at the ground speeding past outside. Even if she managed to not kill herself on landing, she would most certainly be stunned or injured. There was no one around, just a few dark buildings. It would be a simple matter for Davies to turn the car around. The only hard part about it for them would be deciding whether to recapture her or just run her over.

No, if she was going to try jumping she should wait until they were on a street with other traffic at least where someone would see what was happening and be able to help, or, at the bare minimum, call the police.

They drove for another minute before Davies slowed down slightly. "Where do we go?" he asked at last.

"I don't even know where I am," she said, fishing for information.

"You said you could drive to this place," the woman said, turning to glare at her.

"Yes, but not when I don't know my starting point. In fact, I have to retrace the path we took exactly which means we need to start at my Uncle's place for me to be able to take you to where he hid everything."

She held her breath, hoping that they'd buy it.

Davies and the woman exchanged a quick look and then he turned left. "Fine, we will take you to your uncle's house," he said.

Cindy leaned back in her seat, relieved that at least one thing was going her way. There was a good chance there were police officers there who would notice a strange car driving past. While she waited for them to reach a main road she turned and glanced at the door. She still thought jumping might be a good idea. That was when she realized that there were no interior door handles in the backseat.

She scowled. They might be fake law enforcement officers but it seemed like their car was real, or at least a reasonable facsimile. So much for her plan to jump.

She began praying that the streets outside of Heinrich's house were crawling with police.

Daniels picked the lock on a side door and the three officers were inside the building in seconds. Mark's eyes were instantly drawn to a couple of dim lights that seemed to be on at the back of the building.

He motioned to the others and the three fanned out but covered the ground swiftly. Mark kept sweeping his eyes right and left looking for any signs of movement. There was nothing. They finally reached the back of the building. There was a corridor with dim lights burning and a room opening off of it. There was another door as well which was closed.

The room was empty. Liam and Daniels went through the closed door and Mark looked through to see a narrow alley that ran behind the warehouse.

"Tire tracks, someone left in a hurry," Liam noted.

"You can still smell the rubber," Daniels said.

Mark slammed his fist into the wall. They had just missed her, but how?

"Can you track them?" he asked, turning to Daniels.

"Not without my computer. I'd have to get back to the precinct, but even then I'm not sure. There's no guarantee they were driving the van. If it was an entirely different vehicle this could get tricky to say the least.

"How did they know we were coming?" he demanded. "We didn't hear them driving off while we were outside, so they must have left just before we got here."

The other two officers stared at him blankly. Finally Liam cleared his throat. "They could have had surveillance, a silent alarm, something."

"They've been a step ahead of us at every turn. It's like they knew we were coming. It's just like it was when we went to see the art restorer. But this? How did they know? No one knew we were coming here except the three of us and Jeremiah. I swear, I feel like I'm being watched."

Mark yanked his phone out of his pocket. Daniels was staring at him eyes narrowed, when suddenly he reached out and snatched the phone away from him.

"What are you-"

Daniels put a finger up to his lips, indicating the need for silence.

Mark stared at him, wondering what was going on. He watched while Daniels turned the phone off and then handed it back to him.

"What did you do that for?" Mark asked.

"I don't know for sure, but if they're seeming to know things that they shouldn't, it's possible they're spying on us. And if agents of foreign governments really are involved in all of this then it's possible that they force paired your phone so they can eavesdrop on your calls."

"Are you kidding me?" Mark asked.

Daniels shook his head.

"They do it all the time on that *Person of Interest* TV show," Liam pointed out.

"Alright, fine. One of you give me your phone so I can call the rabbi and tell him what's happened and get that description of the kidnappers from him," Mark growled.

It spooked him to think someone might have been listening in on his calls that way. It seemed ridiculous, far-fetched. Then again he had used his phone to call his friend at the F.B.I. the first time and when the kidnappers snatched Cindy they posed as feds. Was that a coincidence or had they heard him make the call and mention that Cindy and Jeremiah knew he was calling them in?

If that were somehow true, though, then he was pretty sure someone other than the Germans had taken Cindy. If they had the ability to listen to his calls they wouldn't have just shown up at the synagogue and left without being a lot more aggressive and knowing who he and Cindy were. After all, Jeremiah had specifically called saying he'd found something.

No, it wasn't possible. But at this stage of the game a little paranoia wouldn't hurt. After all, he'd had his own hacker help in getting them this far in tracking the kidnappers. It was easy to believe the bad guys would be willing to take things a lot farther in order to stay one step ahead and in the loop about what the police knew.

"I hate this case," he muttered.

"What do you think is going on, Detective?" Liam asked, as he handed him his phone. "Who do you think has her?"

"Honestly, I think there are far more pieces on this board than we've seen yet," Mark said. "And that scares the crap out of me."

He took a deep breath, dreading the next thing he had to do, even though he knew it was necessary. He finally forced himself to call Jeremiah and the rabbi picked up on the first ring.

"She's gone. We think she was here, but they moved her right as we got here. I don't know how they knew, but somehow they did."

There was a pause. "Someone eavesdropping on you?"

"Don't say that! Daniels already made that suggestion and frankly it's far too outrageous and too creepy to be true. But, just in case, that's why I'm using Liam's phone. If you need to call me for any reason this will be the phone to reach me on until further notice."

"How do you know she was actually there?"

"Circumstantial evidence at the moment. I'll get some forensic guys down here to see what they can find. Hopefully we can prove she was here and find some DNA giving us identities for her attackers. Now, give me the description of the two goons."

"Male, thirties, tall, dark hair, a scar just above his lip on the right side."

"Doesn't sound like anyone I know," Mark grunted. "And the other?"

"Female, early thirties, long neck, attractive, about 5 foot eight, light blonde hair worn in a severe bun."

In his mind's eye Mark saw the lady from the auction house that Trevor had been talking to when he went to question him more about his father's murder. He shook his head. That was ridiculous. There were dozens of women who could fit that description.

"You know her?" Jeremiah asked sharply.

"Probably not. I saw a blonde that fits that general description the other day, but then, you just described probably a quarter of the aspiring actresses in L.A."

"But this isn't L.A. and if your mind went to her, that's probably significant," Jeremiah said. "Was there something off about her?"

"No, she was just doing her job, worked for an art auction company. She was talking to the son of the dead art dealer from a year ago when I went over to the shop. She didn't say anything to me. When I left she was fiddling with her phone."

"Making a call?" Daniels interjected.

"No, just sort of had it out and was staring at it, like maybe she had a message or something."

"Or maybe she was pairing your phone right in front of you," Daniels said.

That was the last thing Mark wanted to hear.

"It was after that you talked to the art restorer, wasn't it?" Liam asked.

"Yeah. Trevor was the only one who knew I was going to talk to her and I figured he couldn't be stupid enough to voluntarily give me contact information for her and then run over and kill her."

"So, either it was a complete coincidence, or someone else knew you were headed there," Liam said. "Which leaves having your phone conversation with her listened to or having the woman in the store overhear what was going on. Or possibly both.

"The auction lady sounds like a good place to start," Jeremiah growled.

"Alright. I'll call Trevor, see if he's got a number for her," Mark said. "And if she's clean, maybe I can still get her help running down another art expert."

"Good. Now, are you sure there's nothing you can see there where you're at that will help you find Cindy?" Jeremiah pressed.

Mark walked into the one room. It looked like someone had set it up to look like a very crude interrogation room. There were three chairs and a table. "Nothing really here," Mark said and then stopped as his eyes fell on something dark on the far side of the table. "Hold on a second."

He walked around the table and looked down. There, someone had written a word in very small letters in a dark reddish substance that he was guessing was blood. He bent down and sniffed it. It certainly smelled like blood.

"What is it?" Jeremiah asked.

"Someone set up this room to look like an interrogation room. And I found something. If Cindy was here, it looks like she left a message, wrote it in blood," Mark said.

"Blood?" Jeremiah hissed.

"Yeah, don't worry, there's not too much of it."

"What does it say?"

"Captain. Capital C. Does that mean anything to you?"

"Yes, it does."

"You know where they're heading?" Mark asked.

"She's leading them to my house."

Mark swore. "We can't beat them there."

"That's okay," Jeremiah said. "I can."

He hung up and Mark swore again and tossed the phone to Liam. He turned and sprinted for the front of the building, the other two close on his heels.

Cindy had forced her kidnappers to drive to Heinrich's street first, claiming she only knew how to get where they were going by following the route he had driven her on. She was hoping beyond hope that there would be officers present outside the house.

Davies drove to the street, but refused to drive past the house. When she insisted that that was the direction they had gone he backtracked and made a series of sharp turns until they came out on the same road half a block down. He had successfully bypassed the house.

She had wanted to scream in frustration, but had to deal with it. The next decision facing her was just how circuitous a route to take. The faster they made it to Jeremiah's house the faster she could try to escape or call for help. On the other hand, if by some miracle her message was discovered, the longer she could delay the better the chances that officers would be waiting for them at the house when they arrived.

In the end she decided that the odds of someone seeing her message in time were quite small compared with the odds that her captors would get impatient or spooked if she took too long getting them to where Heinrich had supposedly hidden the paintings.

To that end she took them on a fairly direct route to Jeremiah's house, all the while running through different plans in her mind about how she might try to escape or at least get to the phone before they could stop her.

Captain was her ace in the hole. They wouldn't be expecting the German Shepherd. Hopefully he would buy her the time she needed. He was her best hope. That was part of the reason she had written his name on the table. That and she was fairly certain that only an ally would have any chance of deciphering its meaning.

As they neared the final turn Cindy's nerves became more and more frayed. If these people had photographs of her going into her home, it was possible they had photographs of Jeremiah and his home, especially since, unlike her, Jeremiah had actually met Heinrich. She practically held her breath as they turned down his street. If they suspected where she was taking them this would be all over.

"That house," she said, pointing.

"It is not in a storage facility?" Davies asked with a frown.

"Uncle felt that hiding things in houses was safer and less attention getting. That's why he hid some things in his own home. But most of the collection he hid here."

They still seemed to be buying the uncle charade and they didn't seem to recognize the house, both of which boded well for her. She mentally ran through the layout of Jeremiah's house one more time. She just hoped Captain was ready to greet her at the door.

They pulled up outside the house. Cindy noticed that Jeremiah's car was nowhere to be seen. She wondered if that meant her message had been received in time for him or Mark to move it or if Jeremiah had just made it back home on his own, taken his car, and left again.

The other two got out of the car and then Davies opened her door and pulled her out. "Let's see these paintings," he said, his voice tense.

Cindy walked up toward the front door. There were no lights on. "My uncle gave me a key last week, but it's in my purse back at my work," she said.

"It's no matter," Davies said as they stepped up onto the front porch. He turned and kept his eyes on the street which was devoid of movement while the woman extracted something from her pocket, bent over, and began working on the locks.

Thirty seconds later she pushed the door open and they all stepped inside. Davies quickly closed the door behind them.

Cindy strained her ears, listening for the sound of Captain's nails on the floor. There was nothing, though, only silence. Her heart sank. She was going to have to rule out going for the phone in the kitchen since she wouldn't be able to break free of them.

No matter, there was another phone in the house. She could still get out of this, she told herself. And maybe Captain was asleep.

"Show us where he hid the artwork," the woman said.

"It's through here," Cindy said, as loudly as she dared, in the hopes that it would wake the dog. She stepped into the living room.

"Where is the light switch?" Davies growled.

As if by magic the lamp across the room next to the chair turned on. Sitting in the chair was Jeremiah, a gun pointed at them.

18

Cindy gasped and ran toward Jeremiah, careful to stay out of his line of fire.

He stood in one swift motion. "Go to the bedroom and shut the door," he ordered.

She turned in midstride and ran to the room. The door was closed and she turned the knob, opened it just enough to slide inside, and then closed the door again. She then dropped down to the floor in case there was gunfire. Her heart was pounding and she was overwhelmed with relief that she was no longer alone. If Jeremiah had been waiting for them, surely the police were nearby.

She heard a whining sound next to her and she turned to see Captain laying on the ground a few feet away. He wouldn't come any closer even when she called to him. Jeremiah must have ordered him to stay put.

She turned back to stare at the door, straining to hear what was going on in the rest of the house.

Jeremiah stood, staring down the two kidnappers. His first instinct had been to shoot the man on sight just for good measure and leave the woman alive to answer some questions for him and for the police that were surely on their way.

It had taken all of his willpower not to do it. He had worked so hard for so long to keep Cindy from actually seeing him kill anyone. He wasn't sure if he had entirely succeeded, but killing the man like that would have definitely scarred her and that was a risk he just wasn't willing to take.

"First, remove your guns slowly, drop them on the floor and kick them away. Then the three of us are going to have a nice little conversation," Jeremiah said. "Nod if you understand."

They both nodded slowly.

"Okay, first you, lady."

The woman pulled a gun out from the shoulder holster she was wearing under her jacket and dropped it on the floor. She kicked it and sent it skidding underneath the couch.

"Good, your turn," he said, nodding toward the man.

The woman had played it safe. Whether it was because she was scared or was smart enough to realize that she couldn't win this one, he didn't know. The man, on the other hand, had a look in his eyes that he didn't like. He was going to try something.

"Don't do it," Jeremiah warned.

The man reached for the gun slowly, pulled it from its holster, then dove sideways.

Jeremiah fired, shooting him through the heart.

The woman dropped to the floor and reached under the couch in an attempt to retrieve her gun.

"You don't want to die today," he said.

She froze and looked up at him with wide eyes.

"Your partner's gone, so it's just you and I. Why don't you go sit down at the table before I change my mind and decide to kill you, too?"

She swallowed and then very slowly pulled her hand out from under the couch. She stood up, crossed over to the table, and sat down in the same seat Cindy had eaten breakfast in less than twenty-four hours earlier.

"Good. Now, I want you to tell me everything. Let's start with something simple. What's your name?"

"Lisa," she said.

"Okay, I doubt that's the truth, but we'll start there. Now, Lisa, who do you work for?"

Her gaze ticked to the body on the floor.

"No, he was your partner, not your boss. Let's try again. Who do you work for?" Jeremiah asked, taking a step closer and aiming the gun between her eyes.

"I work for myself," she bit out.

"Now that is the first thing you've said that I believe. So, you don't work for a boss, no government, I'm guessing you are very interested in art."

"Who isn't?" she asked.

"I'm also guessing, that you posed as an auction house representative so that you could search the art gallery to see what you could find."

"I figured I'd get an early jump on the bidding, buy a couple of pieces outright," she said flippantly.

Jeremiah studied her carefully. She came across as strong, fearless, but he could see her eyes and he knew the truth. She was terrified. She was just good at putting on a front and fooling people. She'd probably been doing that most of her life.

"How long have you been in town?" he asked.

"A couple of days."

He was going to change up his line of questioning, let her understand that her only defense was to tell him everything she knew.

Just then there was pounding on the front door. She jumped and turned wide eyes that direction.

There was someone she was far more afraid of than him and she was worried he was the one at the door.

"Come in!" Jeremiah called.

"Wait, you don't know who that might be," she said.

"It's the police," he told her as the door flew open and Mark ran inside followed by two other officers.

She relaxed noticeably when she saw them.

Mark had his gun out and he stared at Jeremiah in surprise. His eyes swept the area and quickly took in the dead body on the floor. "Where's Cindy?" he asked.

"Bedroom. She'd probably appreciate it if someone would get the handcuffs off of her."

"I'm on it," Liam said as he headed back toward the bedroom.

Less than a minute later he reappeared with Cindy who was pale but appeared unharmed. She was shaking out her hands, clearly relieved to be freed from her restraints.

Captain wasn't with her. He was impressed the dog had been able to restrain himself and obey orders so long. He'd have to reward him with something extra special later.

"Jeremiah, we've got this," Mark said finally. "You can put down the gun."

"Not until you check her for other weapons and handcuff her. You'll find her gun under the couch where she kicked it."

"Okay," Mark said, eyeing him warily.

Liam searched the woman and then handcuffed her while the officer Jeremiah didn't recognize fished the gun out from under the couch. When both tasks were done, Jeremiah slid his gun into the back of his waistband.

Mark turned to the third officer. "Daniels, go search the car outside and see if you can find anything. Make sure you wear gloves."

The man nodded and left.

"You okay?" Mark asked, turning to look at Cindy. She nodded.

"Good. Okay, now let's get down to the bottom of this," Mark said, pulling out a chair and taking a seat at the table. He waved Jeremiah toward a chair.

"I'll stand for a while longer," Jeremiah said.

"Okay, someone catch me up," Mark said.

Cindy pointed to the woman. "She and a guy kidnapped me."

"Is that the guy?" Mark asked, pointing to the body.

She turned to look and her face grew ashen. She clearly hadn't noticed the body until just that moment.

"Yes," she said, her eyes flying to Jeremiah. He didn't give any confirmation that he was the one who had shot the man though that clearly had to be what she suspected. She wasn't stupid. It had been quite a long time between the gunshot and Liam letting her out of the room.

"They pretended to be F.B.I. and kidnapped me from the church."

"We figured that out when Wildman called," Mark said.

"Oh, thank goodness," she said. Then she hesitated for a moment. "Was he the only one who called you?"

"Yes," Jeremiah said, knowing she was wondering why Roy hadn't said anything. He'd probably have to talk to her about that later.

"Who are they really?" she asked, rubbing her wrists which had red marks on them.

"That's what we're hoping to find out," Mark said.

Cindy sat down on the couch. "They had a bunch of photos of Heinrich. They'd been following him for weeks. The weird thing was, I was in a lot of those pictures because apparently he was following me."

"He was following you?" Jeremiah asked. That seemed odd. "Are you sure they were real and not just photoshopped?"

"I honestly don't know. One of them at least was real. It was a picture of me sitting on a bench at the park resting while you and Captain were playing fetch. Heinrich was sitting next to me. I hadn't even remembered that until I saw the picture."

Jeremiah leaned forward. He hadn't seen Heinrich in the park. He hadn't seen him since that day at the synagogue back in May until he'd been standing over his dead body a few days ago. "Did he say anything to you in the park?"

"They asked me the same thing," Cindy said. "I finally remembered sitting next to him. He was watching you and Captain play. And he said 'he seems like a good man.' I wasn't sure if he was actually talking to me or even talking about you. I said, 'yes, he is," in case he was. That was it. He got up and left."

"That was what, about three weeks ago?" Jeremiah asked.

Cindy nodded.

Had Heinrich been following him as well without his knowing it? The thought terrified him. How could he have missed something like that? He felt himself break out into a cold sweat.

Daniels came in from outside. "I did a quick search. I found these in the front seat, nothing else," he said, putting a phone and a folder down on the table. He handed Mark an extra pair of gloves which the Detective slipped on before flipping open the folder.

"Looks like some of those pictures you were talking about, Cindy." He pulled one out and showed it to Jeremiah. It was indeed Cindy and Heinrich sitting together on a bench in the park.

Jeremiah shook his head. Clearly he had been too busy playing with Captain to notice. That wasn't a good sign at all.

Next Mark picked up the phone. He pushed a few buttons and frowned. "Some of these numbers seem awfully familiar."

Jeremiah glanced at the woman. She looked cornered. "Something wrong?" he asked her.

"Hold on," Daniels said. "Detective, turn your phone back on. I'm going to call it."

Mark pulled out his phone and turned it on. A moment later Daniels called it. Mark's phone rang and so did the one on the desk. He answered his phone and then the other one. A look of fury settled on his face.

"You! You paired my phone. It was you who killed the art restorer," he shouted.

No wonder she had looked cornered when the phone was discovered, Jeremiah realized.

"I want to talk to a lawyer," the woman said.

"I'm afraid that won't help you much," a voice said from the front door which Daniels had left open.

Jeremiah glanced up. Albert, the German who had visited him in his office, was standing there, filling the doorway.

Mark jumped to his feet, drawing his weapon, and training it on the German. His mind raced, wondering what the man was doing there and where his compatriots were at that moment.

"It's okay, Detective," Albert said.

"Sit down, Mark. It's fine," Jeremiah said, his voice completely calm and unruffled.

"What is he doing here?" Mark asked.

"I invited him," Jeremiah said. "We had a nice phone conversation wherein he admitted to me who he really is."

"And that would be?" Cindy asked.

"BKA," Jeremiah said.

"For those of us playing at home that would be, what?" Mark asked.

"Bundeskriminalamt," Albert said.

"Still not helpful," Mark said, feeling his temper begin to slip.

"The Federal Criminal Police Office of Germany," Jeremiah supplied. "They handle cases related to international organized crime and terrorism among other things."

"So, you're a cop," Mark said.

"Essentially," Albert said.

"Then let's see your identification."

Albert pulled a piece of paper out of his coat pocket. Liam stepped forward and looked it over. "That's what it says," he confirmed.

Mark slowly holstered the weapon.

"Why not tell us that up front?"

"You have to understand, the theft of art and cultural treasures is a very...sensitive subject. And it is hard to know who you can trust, who is involved and who isn't. Until I knew more about the situation, I couldn't risk revealing myself to anyone."

"So, instead you just came off as a thug. What were you trying to do?" Mark said.

"I was hoping that if you were involved you would think of me as either a corrupt politician or someone involved with the antiquities black market."

"Corrupt politician had my vote," Mark admitted.

"I thought you were some sort of spy or something doing dark things for your country," Cindy said.

He smiled. "While it is regrettable that the type of man you are describing is a necessary evil in this world, I am not one of those."

"So, what are you doing in southern California?" Cindy asked.

"I've been here for several months. We received a tip from an art dealer here in Pine Springs. His father used to be a part of the black market trade, but he was not. His specialty was art restoration and although he did not traffic in high-end art, he did recognize a piece that a customer brought in to have him clean. Apparently someone had carelessly spilled some paint on it.

"He contacted us, and told us he believed it to be a piece that once belonged to a museum in Berlin, a Rubens, one of his pieces on the Conversion of St. Paul, thought destroyed in a fire in 1945. He was advised that investigators would have to be sent out to authenticate the piece, but he was concerned about the tight deadline the customer had given him and as he did not know the man's last name or contact information he was afraid the piece would be lost.

"So, he told us that he had painted over the picture with something innocuous to hide it."

"The dogs playing poker," Cindy said.

"And then he switched it for a copy that he hoped would pass inspection, at least until the authorities could get involved."

"Which clearly didn't work since we didn't find the copy, but we did find the original, painted over, wrapped in a blood splattered package," Cindy said.

Albert nodded. "By the time I and an authentication expert made it out here, he was already dead and there was no sign of the Rubens."

Mark hunched his shoulders, feeling his irritation level rising even higher. "I was one of the detectives working that homicide. You know, if you had come to me then maybe we could have saved everyone a lot of trouble and there'd be a few people alive today that aren't."

"Perhaps. I couldn't risk alerting the killer to my presence, though. And, when I got here, I discovered that someone did not know how to keep their mouth shut. It was either someone the art dealer knew or someone working in my office. It seems I was not the only one who had heard that a lost Rubens had been discovered."

He nodded to the woman. "Her name is Katrina Gregorovich. She has long been known to us as an art thief, but we have never had anything we could actually pin on her without a doubt. That is, until today thanks to her and her partner growing desperate and kidnapping you." he said, looking at Cindy.

"Yay," Cindy said with a grimace. "So glad I could help."

Mark couldn't help but wonder if the level of sarcasm she was expressing was lost in translation since Albert quite sincerely said, "We appreciate your assistance in this matter greatly."

"She's Russian," Jeremiah said.

"*Ja.*"

"You said it was possible there was a Russian connection. It's just not quite what we had in mind," Mark noted.

The rabbi nodded slowly, but didn't say anything.

"Now that we have her in custody and she's facing a very long prison sentence for murder, kidnapping, and anything else we can make stick, I'm sure she'll be more than willing to cooperate with us and tell us where she has stashed the Rubens she stole."

Katrina snarled, all defiance, but Mark was pretty sure she would cave once Albert got her to Germany. That is, if he was allowed to leave with her. She had committed the murders and the kidnapping here in this country. At least that was something he didn't have to sort out. It was above his pay grade and he was glad of it.

"We do have another Rubens that we found. Heinrich clearly realized someone was about to kill him when he got rid of it," Jeremiah said.

"That is a wonderful thing then," Albert said.

Mark noticed Jeremiah left out the fact that he'd had it hidden in the closet of his office when Albert had paid him his little visit.

"Why did she kill Heinrich? She and her partner were desperate to figure out where he stashed his stuff. They'd been clearly following him for a while. Why not wait a little longer?" Cindy asked.

"That's a question for her," Albert said. "What happened, Katrina. Did you grow tired of waiting for the old man to lead you to his treasures?"

"I didn't kill him," she hissed.

"So, your partner then?"

"No. He would have led us to the art eventually. All we had to do was wait and we were prepared to wait as long as we had to."

"So, you deny killing him but not the art restorer? Interesting," Mark said. "Strange, but interesting."

"I didn't kill Heinrich," she insisted.

"If not you, then who?" Jeremiah asked.

"I don't know."

"She's lying," Albert said. "No matter. We will soon find out all we need to from her, including who tipped her off about the painting in the first place."

"Heinrich kills Haverston because of the painting. Katrina kills the art restorer and steals the painting. Presumably she or her partner killed Heinrich as well.

"And then someone shot and killed her partner," Albert said.

"That would be me," Jeremiah said.

Mark saw Cindy jerk and turn to stare at Jeremiah. She had to have guessed that already, though.

"I guess it's all over then," Liam said.

Mark started to nod.

Cindy blinked at him. "Nothing's over. We still don't know where any of the rest of the art, if there is any, might be. And then there's the Amber Room."

Albert held up his hand. "Better you leave that to the authorities, the experts, *ja*?"

She folded her arms across her chest. "I'll leave it alone if you can tell me one thing."

"What's that?"

"Who shot Jeremiah?"

Cindy continued to stare at Albert, but he just looked at her with a blank expression. "When was he shot?" he finally asked.

She turned and stared at Katrina who shook her head. "I do not know who shot him."

Cindy looked at Mark whose brow was furrowed. Next she turned to Jeremiah whose face was like a mask.

She cleared her throat. "You see, this isn't over yet. There's someone else out there and they're willing to kill to protect their identity."

"At least two people," Jeremiah said quietly. "The shooter wasn't the one driving the car."

248

Cindy set her jaw. "Until they're brought to justice this is anything but over and we are all still in danger."

Everyone just sat, staring around the room at each other. "Don't you see?" she demanded. "We're only partway there. And Katrina here has at least one other partner. There was a third man wherever it was they were holding me. Just who was he?"

"My bodyguard," Katrina spoke up.

"Where is he now?" Albert demanded.

Jeremiah's eyes shot to the door. Cindy saw something arcing through the air and a moment later there was a brilliant burst of light accompanied by a deafening explosion.

19

Mark's head felt like it was going to explode. Pain seared through him but he couldn't see or hear anything. He felt like he was tilting to the side, dizzy like he'd just got off the teacup ride at Disneyland that Traci loved so much.

Traci.

He was never going to see her again. He struggled to push himself up to a standing position, but he wasn't sure he was succeeding. Something slammed into him and he toppled farther over, falling endlessly, until it seemed like he'd been falling forever.

He hit the ground hard, striking his head a moment after his shoulder, and he was sure he cried out, but he couldn't hear anything. Something kicked his leg and then a moment later something heavy landed on top of him. He felt something hot and warm spilling all over the back of his shirt.

He tried to sit up, but whatever was on top of him was pressing him down. He shouted, but still couldn't hear a thing.

Then, suddenly, his vision and hearing returned, flooding him with sensory input. He was laying on the floor, his head an inch away from the leg of the table. He could hear shouting around him, a high pitched scream that he was guessing was Cindy.

He struggled to sit up, still dizzy and disoriented. He turned to see what it was that had fallen on him and realized that it was Daniels. He had been stabbed in the throat. It had been his blood that he'd felt running down his shirt. His eyes were frozen open in death.

Mark shouted and scrambled out from underneath him. The man's body flopped onto the ground. He looked around frantically. Liam and Albert were slowly sitting up. Cindy was on her knees, swaying slightly. Both Katrina and Jeremiah were gone.

He heard a roar coming from the back of the house and a minute later a streak of fur and fangs went hurtling past him and out the front door.

"Captain!" Cindy shrieked and grabbing the edge of the table hauled herself to her feet. She tried to chase after the dog, staggered, hit the wall, bounced off it and kept going to the front door.

Liam reached out to stop her, but she brushed him off and made it outside.

"Flashbang grenade," Albert said, hauling himself to his feet.

"I bet you didn't see that coming," Mark said, even more angry at the German than he was at himself. "Now our killer is gone, two civilians, too, and a good officer is dead."

"No, you are right. This took me by surprise as much as it did you," Albert said shrewdly.

It was official. Mark hated the man. He reached for his phone and swore when he realized that Katrina's was missing.

"Liam, call it in," he said.

"Where are you going?" Liam asked as Mark weaved his way toward the door.

"To find Cindy and Jeremiah, what else do I ever do?"

As it turned out he didn't have far to go. Cindy was standing at the edge of the lawn staring up the street. There, walking toward them was Jeremiah, with the dog at his side.

"What happened?" Mark questioned when Jeremiah reached them.

"I lost them. I got a license plate, but I'm guessing the car was stolen," Jeremiah said.

And just his luck the one guy that had a chance of tracking down the car was dead.

"How did you get on your feet so fast compared to the rest of us?"

"It was only a second, it probably just felt like longer," Jeremiah said, heading into the house.

As soon as they were all inside Mark made a point of closing the door behind them. He turned and saw Jeremiah staring down at Daniels, his face inscrutable.

"Sorry," he said finally.

"He was a good man," Mark said with a growl.

Within minutes there were police crawling all over Jeremiah's home. It was more than irritating, but he sat on the couch next to Cindy, his arm around her, and watched the proceedings.

"I'm so tired," she whispered.

"I know."

His arm felt like it was on fire. He refused to take any medication for it because he had started using the pain to help remain alert and focused.

"I still think there's someone else out there we don't know about," she said.

"Me, too."

"What are we supposed to do about that?"

He sighed. "We should probably let the police handle it."

"Yes, because they've been doing such a good job so far," she said.

He didn't say anything, just rubbed her shoulder. She leaned her head against him and he could feel her relax ever so slightly.

"There's no way I'm going into work tomorrow," she said.

"There's no way I can't," he sighed.

Finally Mark came over and sat down on Cindy's other side. "So, the three of us agree this isn't over," he said very softly.

Jeremiah nodded.

"Right, there are a couple of killers on the loose. I want both of you to stay somewhere else until this is resolved."

"Like where?" Cindy murmured.

"I've already worked it out. I'm going to send you to stay at Joseph's. Your roommate, too, until this is done. He upgraded his security system last year. That entire place is probably safer than Fort Knox at this point. I've got a couple of officers to volunteer to stand guard as well."

"I have to go to the synagogue tomorrow," Jeremiah said.

"And since I knew you were going to be stubborn about that, I've got one who's going to be hanging around the synagogue tomorrow."

"Great, a babysitter," Jeremiah muttered. "No way to keep that secret from the congregation."

"Better than them finding out the hard way, like you getting killed in the middle of services. Now, grab what you need. I'm going to personally drive you both up there so I know you're safe."

A few minutes later they were settled in the back of Mark's car with Captain laying on the seat between them, his head on Jeremiah's leg. Cindy was asleep within a couple of minutes, but Jeremiah stared out the windows the entire drive, making sure that no one was following them.

When they finally turned up the hill to Joseph's estate he was satisfied that no one had been watching them. They pulled up out front and Geanie ran outside and practically pulled Cindy out of the car. The two women embraced tightly as Jeremiah shook Joseph's hand and Captain stood by his side.

"Thanks for this."

"No problem. The three of you are more than welcome," Joseph said as he bent down to scratch Captain behind the ears. "The guest rooms are all ready and you can stay as long as you need to."

Jeremiah just hoped that their presence didn't put Joseph in danger, too.

It was almost noon when Cindy woke up. She rolled over and looked at the clock, blinking in shock as she saw the time. She stretched and got out of bed. She brushed her teeth and got dressed. She opened her bedroom door to find Captain laying outside it. He looked up at her and whined. She reached down and scratched his chin.

"Rough night, boy?" she asked.

She headed down the long hallway, marveling as she always did, at Joseph's family mansion. She finally made it to the stairs and Captain followed her down. She found Geanie and Joseph in the kitchen making lunch.

"There you are!" Geanie said brightly.

"I guess I was really out of it," Cindy said sheepishly.

"We all were. It was a long, stressful night for everyone," Joseph said. "I didn't get up until around ten."

"I was up even later," Geanie said. "I'm in the room with that beautiful red canopy bed. The mattress was so soft I didn't want to ever get up."

Cindy smiled to herself. Geanie was marrying Joseph in a few short months but it hadn't yet hit her that this was going to be her mansion, too, when that happened.

"Yeah, Jeremiah was the only one up early. The officer outside told me that his partner drove him in to work just before eight."

"He must be about to collapse," Cindy murmured, feeling sorry for him. He had to get through today and tomorrow full of services before he'd catch a break for a day or two.

"I called in to work for you," Cindy said. "Sylvia said to take as much time as you need."

"Anything else?"

"Yeah, she tried talking me into coming back to work," Geanie said, wrinkling her nose up. "I told her no, but I did agree to go in after this is all over and do an exit interview, fill out some paperwork and stuff."

An exit interview, that should be interesting, Cindy thought, wondering what exactly Geanie would say.

Mark was not having a good morning. He had done his best to get some sleep, but he kept waking up screaming and seeing Daniels' face. He knew it wasn't his fault, but he still couldn't help but think that he'd gotten the other man killed by involving him in everything.

He had finally given up around six in the morning and driven into the precinct. He had pored over all his notes again, struggling to figure out who Jeremiah's assailant had been.

Albert had said the night before that it was clear that somebody had tipped off Katrina about the painting, either someone in his organization or someone connected to Haverston. Whoever that was, they might be behind Jeremiah's shooting.

He thought of what Katrina had said about Haverston's father having been involved with the black market. He and Paul had heard that rumor back when they were investigating Haverston's murder. There had been allegations, but never any proof. Whoever the old man had been connected to had been very discrete and it was equally clear that his son had worked to distance himself from those connections when he took over the business. Given that he'd called the authorities over the painting it was unlikely that he'd had a change of heart and also called in his father's black market contacts.

But it was entirely possible that someone else had known what he'd found or overheard him talking to the Germans and taken matters into their own hands. Possibly an employee, or a son who thought the grandfather's way of doing business had been better.

Mark blinked. He didn't like Trevor. Was he jumping to him because it was the right conclusion or because it was the satisfying one? He started in on his sixth pot of coffee and contemplated the facts as he knew them.

Whoever had shot Jeremiah had been in a car with diplomatic plates. Since Albert claimed it wasn't him or anyone at the German consulate, that meant there were other international players involved. That screamed black market and high end merchandise to him. Was that who Trevor's grandfather could have worked with? It was easier for diplomats to smuggle things out of the country than it was for U.S. citizens. If that was the case, though, was Katrina, herself Russian, working with the others or were they competitors? She had genuinely seemed to have no knowledge regarding Jeremiah's being shot. That didn't mean, though, that her confederates hadn't just left her in the dark on that.

He called Liam from his desk phone. When the other officer answered he said, "Yeah, can you meet me downtown at Haverston & Sons art gallery right now?"

"Sure. I'll be there as fast as I can."

"Perfect. Stay outside, don't go in without me unless you see something strange."

"Understood."

Mark took another swallow of coffee and then headed for the door.

Jeremiah staggered into his office. There had finally been a break in the services, which was a blessing because he was just about to drop. He closed his eyes and tried to still his mind. He had to pay such close attention during the service that he hadn't had a chance to really focus on G-d, particularly since he'd been paranoid that he would mess up because he was so tired.

He unlocked the bottom drawer of his desk and pulled his gun out. He slid it into the back of his waistband. He had brought it with him, aware that killers were still on the loose, but he hadn't been able to bring himself to take it into the synagogue.

He glanced at the clock. He was expecting Albert any minute. He'd made arrangements with him the night before to surrender the Rubens he had to him. Frankly he'd feel a lot better when it was out of his hands and no longer his responsibility.

He would be lying to himself, though, if he didn't admit to having mixed emotions. His mother carried a hatred for the German people still for what the Nazis had done. She understood intellectually that the people who had done those terrible things were for the most part dead and gone and that the younger generations couldn't be blamed for the sins of their elders. Still, he understood where the anger came from.

And given all the art treasures stolen from the Jews by the Nazis, hundreds of thousands of which were still missing, it was indeed bitter sweet that the one he had found legitimately belonged to the German museum and wasn't something that would be restored to one of his people.

Restoration.

That was the word Heinrich had written in his own blood with his dying breath. Had he known that the paintings didn't belong to the Jewish people? Had he wanted them returned to their proper owners whoever those turned out to be?

And why was it he had come to services that day and so urgently wanted to talk to him? Had the presence of Katrina or others in town prevented him from ever trying to connect again?

Jeremiah pressed his fingers against his head. There were too many questions still, ones that would likely never be answered. Life was like that, though. One rarely got answers wrapped in neat little bundles with all the loose ends tied in bows. Life was messy and complicated and left all sorts of unresolved issues.

Like what he was going to do about Cindy.

He sighed, got up and retrieved the painting from where he had hidden it underneath the couch. It hadn't been the world's greatest hiding place, but he hadn't had time to do better.

He propped it up face first against the couch so that the back was facing him. He stared again at the second string of numbers, wondering what exactly they meant. Had Heinrich put them there or some museum cataloguer?

There was a knock on his door.

"Come in," he said, wearily.

Marie opened the door. "There's a German man here to see you," she said, her lips in a tight, disapproving line.

"Thanks, you can go ahead and send him in," Jeremiah said, returning his eyes to the back of the painting.

Marie followed his gaze. "What are you staring at?"

"I'm trying to figure out what that bottom string of numbers means," he said. There was no need to hide that or the painting itself any more. The painting would be gone in moments.

"They look like coordinates to me," Marie said.

Jeremiah looked up sharply. "What do you mean?"

"Coordinates, like GPS. My sister and her husband do that geocaching thing, you know?"

"No, I don't know," Jeremiah said.

"It's this big thing, millions of people all over the world do it. You take a small box say and you hide it somewhere like under a log in a forest or in some bushes in a park and you leave a log book so that whoever finds it can record their name. Some of them even include small gifts that people can exchange. It's usually just small stuff. Up in northern California, though, they once found one that had rubies in it. Anyway, you hide the cache, log the coordinates on a website, and then people try to find it. It's like a big treasure hunt basically. They took us once. We didn't find any rubies, but it was at least an interesting afternoon. Anyway, that looks like coordinates to me."

"Marie, you're a genius," Jeremiah said as he got to his feet. "An absolute genius."

"I've been telling you that for years," she said tartly.

She left his office and he stood in the doorway. Albert was walking toward him. Jeremiah waved to him impatiently then stepped back. "There's your Rubens," he said, pointing. "Take it."

"Are you in a hurry?" Albert asked, looking surprised.

"Yes, I am."

Jeremiah pushed his way past him and into the outer office. "Marie, how much time do I have?"

"About another hour and a half, why?"

"I'll be back," he said, racing out the door.

"Where are you going?" she shouted.

He got into his car, pulled up the picture he had taken before of the back of the painting and punched the coordinates into his GPS app. Then he called Cindy.

"How are you doing?" she asked.

"Want to go on a treasure hunt?" he said, not bothering to answer her question.

"Sure."

"I'm heading for a set of coordinates, meet me there."

He gave them to her then hung up the phone and began to drive. Fifteen minutes later he was pulling up outside a cemetery. He climbed out of his car just as Cindy, Joseph, and Geanie arrived in Joseph's car.

"What are we looking for?" Cindy asked breathlessly as she ran up to him.

"The second set of numbers on the back of the Rubens. I think they're coordinates."

"That direction!" Geanie said, consulting a phone and then pointing into the heart of the cemetery. "It says we're about a quarter of a mile away."

The four of them set off across the grass, turning slightly as the GPS indicated.

"100 feet, we're getting close," Geanie said.

"What is it we're looking for exactly?" Joseph said.

"I don't know, I'm hoping we'll know it when we see it," Jeremiah said.

"Twenty feet. We should be on top of it any moment."

Jeremiah stopped and looked around. There, a few feet away was a massive crypt. He walked up to it and read the inscription on it. "Einigkeit und Recht und Freiheit."

"What does that mean?" Cindy asked.

"Unity and Justice and Freedom, it's the official motto of Germany."

"So, you think this belonged to Heinrich?" she asked.

Jeremiah crouched down. "I'd say so. This carving is much newer." He pointed to a small Star of David on the door.

"What do we do now?" Joseph asked. He picked up the chain that was holding the door closed and examined the lock on it. "I guess we need to call the police and wait for them. They'll probably have to get some sort of court order to open it."

"Stand back," Jeremiah said.

The others moved a couple of feet back. He pulled the gun out of his waistband and they hastily retreated much farther. He aimed it at the lock and fired.

He replaced the gun, and took the now shattered lock off the chain. "Shall we?" he asked.

Cindy nodded, her eyes wide.

Together they pulled open the door and stepped inside. Light filtered through the doorway, pale and weak. Then a much brighter light stabbed the darkness as Cindy held up her phone. "Flashlight app," she said.

They stepped into the crypt, Joseph and Geanie right behind them. A few more steps in and Jeremiah stopped in his tracks. Next to him he could hear Cindy gasp.

There, in front of them, was row after row of stacked paintings, each wrapped in a protective sheath.

"It's true," Cindy whispered. "He got them out, before the fire."

"Yes."

"How many do you think there are? One hundred and thirteen?"

He shook his head. "I think he got *all* of them out." He cleared his throat. "Now I think it's time to call the police."

Mark got out of his car and joined Liam on the sidewalk a few stores down from the art gallery. Liam handed him his phone. "Jeremiah called, you'll want to call him back."

"After."

Liam shook his head, his eyes wide. "I don't think it will wait."

Mark called and the rabbi picked up instantly.

"What is so important it can't wait ten minutes?" Mark asked.

"We found the rest of the paintings. *All* of them," Jeremiah said.

"Tell me where you are."

As soon as Jeremiah had given him directions Mark hung up and called dispatch. He explained that he had a situation he was in the middle of, but that he needed officers to arrest Trevor Haverston and to look for anything that would connect him with Russians. As soon as he was finished he grabbed Liam and the two of them headed for the cemetery.

Adrenalin was still pumping through Cindy as she, Joseph and Geanie left the cemetery, ordered out by Mark and Albert, whom Jeremiah had called second after Mark. Both men had shown up to take charge of the paintings and the entire situation. Jeremiah had left immediately after their arrival to return to the synagogue.

Cindy knew that for the rest of her life she'd never forget the site of those stacks and stacks of paintings. Hundreds of millions of dollars was what Jeremiah had said it must all be worth. It was unreal. Deep down she was furious that she'd had to leave before everything was resolved with them.

Then again, Mark had pointed out it would probably be months before things were truly resolved with them. Governments would have to be involved, negotiations, all sorts of things.

"That was incredible," Geanie was gushing. "I never dreamed we'd find hidden treasure like that."

"It was unreal," Joseph said.

"Buried, just like what the Nazis did with so many treasure troves," Cindy mused.

At least she'd gotten to take a good look before the officers had arrived. The one thing she'd been quick to note, though, was that there seemed to be no other pieces of the Amber Room, and that bothered her.

At least now, though, with the artwork found she and Jeremiah wouldn't have to be looking over their shoulders every moment waiting for Katrina or Jeremiah's unknown assailant to find them.

They all headed back to Joseph's house, the other two talking excitedly, but Cindy was too lost in thought to join in. She couldn't shake the feeling that they were still missing something, something very, very important.

20

By the time Mark made it back to the precinct he had nearly forgotten about Trevor. The moment he walked in, though, the captain called him over.

"Good call on the Haverston kid. We did some checking. Seems he learned a few things from his grandfather that they didn't teach him in his fancy business school. He overheard his father talking about the painting he'd found and thought he'd take advantage of it. We applied a little pressure and he rolled on his black market contacts who, it turns out, have ties to someone in the Russian consulate in L.A. They're the ones who got the bright idea of forcing the old man to talk instead of waiting around to see if he'd lead them to anything."

"So, all is explained," Mark said, feeling as though it were a bit anti-climactic. Then again, anything after going through and trying to catalogue hundreds of millions of dollars of missing art would be.

"We've turned everything we have over to the Feds, including the kid. We can wash our hands of the whole mess now."

"Did they ever find Katrina and her bodyguard?"

"No, but it's their problem now, let it alone," his captain advised.

Mark nodded wearily.

Jeremiah made it back to the synagogue just in time. After that service he returned to his office. Only one more service and then the day was done. He wished he knew how things had turned out finally at the crypt. He reached for his phone to call Cindy, but his eyes fell on the videocamera sitting next to his computer.

He guessed the whole thing was kind of moot now. He picked up the camera and turned it on. He glanced at the first segment of video. Not having to walk up and down the wall made it much easier to read. Without having to translate verbatim for the digital recorder it was also much faster.

A minute later he found himself skimming through, able to go at a much faster pace. He read about how Heinrich had partnered with some Russian and American soldiers to get the treasures out of the tower and then out of the country. These same partners he'd later had a falling out with and killed.

He talked of the efforts he had gone to to hide his treasures in America and of having to move them once across the country. He talked of settling in Pine Springs and building a house. He said he had to relocate his treasures, but he never said exactly what he had or where he was putting it.

Then, slowly, he began to talk of a change that came over him. Age and time to reflect eventually stirred guilt in him for all that he had done and a deep desire to make things right. He had taught himself Hebrew. He'd even tried to figure out if anything he owned had been stolen from Jews and which ones, but without revealing anything to other people he couldn't go very far down that road.

One of the paintings had become damaged and he had taken it to an art restorer. Then he believed that the man was trying to steal it. They had fought and ultimately Heinrich had killed him. The guilt added to what he already felt for everything else had nearly destroyed him.

It wasn't long after that he realized the art dealer must have told others about what he had. Heinrich wrote about his growing paranoia that he was being watched, followed. He felt his days were drawing to a close and he just wanted to find a way to make things right. Then he found a synagogue with a nice rabbi who was actually from Israel.

Jeremiah halted, hitting pause on the video. Him. Heinrich was recounting his meeting with him. He finally hit play again and continued to read, more closely now.

Heinrich had had every intention of keeping their meeting and revealing his secret and begging Jeremiah for his help in what he was starting to think of as the Great Restoration. When he headed for the synagogue, though, he discovered beyond a shadow of a doubt that he was not paranoid, but that people were looking for the paintings. He didn't dare risk meeting the rabbi lest they guess his plans.

He began to follow the girl that spent so much time with the rabbi hoping that he could make contact that way. His one chance in the park was again ruined by someone following him.

The last few lines were hurried, sloppy, something had changed and he knew that his stalkers had grown tired of waiting and that a confrontation was imminent. He was going to leave something behind, that only the one chosen by G-d could use and that all would be well and the Great Restoration would go forward, even if he wasn't alive to see it.

Jeremiah sat, stunned, when he came to the end of the narrative. Restoration. The last thought on the old man's mind.

Marie knocked on his door, startling him. "Time," she said.

Cindy was sitting in Joseph's living room, her hand still wrapped around her cell. Mark had called to update her on everything he had learned. She'd scarcely hung up with him when Jeremiah did the same.

It was over as far as both men were concerned. But she still couldn't let it go. Not without one last look at the house where this had all started. She called them both back and they agreed to meet her at Heinrich's home later that evening.

She was the last to arrive. Both Mark and Jeremiah were inside, comparing notes. They both looked as tired as she felt. She clearly had come into the middle of the conversation.

"Doesn't it strike you as odd that the contractor and three of the guys who helped build this house died just as it was being completed?" Jeremiah asked. "Heinrich didn't mention anything about that in his description of having the house built."

"Yes, but you know what strikes me as more odd? In this entire place there was only a nail hole in one wall. All of the walls look pristine, like they've never been touched, patched, anything," Cindy added.

"Well, he clearly was only really living in the one room," Mark said.

"And he had a priceless piece of the Amber Room under the floor. Where did the rest of it go?" Cindy asked.

"I don't know. Isn't it enough we found all those paintings?" Mark asked. "The bad guys have gone to jail, art has been recovered. Can't we just call the case closed and let someone else somewhere down the road worry about the Amber Room? I mean, for all we know the piece we found is the only piece he was able to smuggle out of Germany."

"It's possible," Jeremiah said with a shrug.

"It's over, Cindy, let it go," Mark said. "We've all earned a rest."

Cindy didn't like it. The location of the rest of the panels from that room was going to drive her crazy, she just knew it.

"Have either of you got a hammer or something?" Cindy asked as a thought occurred to her.

"No," Jeremiah said.

"Sorry, why?" Mark asked.

"I'll be right back," Cindy said, heading for the front door.

She made it outside, opened her trunk, and grabbed her tire iron. She hefted it in her hand. She slammed the trunk closed and headed back inside the house.

Both men had walked closer to the door and took a step back when she walked in.

"What exactly are you planning on doing with that?" Mark asked.

"I'll show you," she said, marching toward the bedroom.

She walked up to one of the walls, ran her hand along it, then took a step back. She wrapped both her hands around the tire iron and then swung it like a baseball bat.

Both guys shouted as the tire iron made contact with the wall. The iron went right through and slivers of wood rained down.

Mark bent down and grabbed one of them. "This is just painted balsa wood. You wouldn't make walls out of this. What on earth?"

"Not real walls," Cindy said, grabbing an edge and breaking it off.

There, behind the false wall, she caught a glint of something. She stepped back and handed the tire iron to Mark.

"What is it?" he asked.

"I just figured out what Heinrich did with the rest of the Amber Room."

Less than five minutes later Mark and Jeremiah had torn down the rest of the wall. There, resting right behind it, was another section of the famed wall, amber and jewels glittering in the light.

They made quick work of the rest of the walls in the room, finding the same behind each of them.

"I'm betting he had false walls installed in every room, with the possible exception of that one wall in the dining room that actually had something hanging on it," Cindy said. "He hid the room where he could always keep an eye on it."

"And then he killed the four men who helped him do it and made it look like a car accident," Mark realized. "That's insane."

"It was ingenious," Jeremiah said.

"We're going to have to take this entire house down to its foundations before we're through," Mark said. "Who knows what else he hid where." He looked at Cindy. "How did you know?"

"Just a feeling, a lucky guess. He hid most of the paintings offsite, but he had that one piece of the room close to him. He felt guilt about the paintings because he felt somehow they were stolen from the Jewish people, whether they were or not. But not the Amber Room. The Amber Room was stolen from the Russians and I'm guessing he didn't care nearly as much about them."

Mark sighed. "I'm calling my friend at the Bureau. I'm not even about to try and sort this one out."

Cindy nodded, a feeling of peace settling over her. She looked at both men. "Now, now it's over," she whispered.

Just over a week later Mark was sitting in his captain's office with a feeling of dread eating away at his insides. He'd been waiting for fifteen minutes when the man finally entered, closed the door and took a seat behind his desk.

He studied something on his desk for a moment and then glanced up. "How are you doing?"

"Better. Caught up on a lot of sleep," Mark said.

"Good."

The man looked down at something on his desk again and then shifted in his chair.

"I've been told by the mayor that the German government is officially requesting that you be given a citation for bravery and going above and beyond the call of duty. Apparently they're also planning on some sort of official awards from the German government for those involved in this whole mess."

Mark blinked in surprise. "Sir?"

"I know. I'm right there with you. Bottom line is, I've been told to treat you like a freaking hero."

"I don't know what to say."

"Neither do I. So, let's get down to business. I need to assign you a new partner. We've got an odd number of detectives currently so that means either bringing someone in or promoting someone up."

"I'd like to make a suggestion in that regard," Mark said.

"After having read your report I'm not surprised. He's going to need a lot of training still."

"Yes, but he's a good man and he'll make a great detective."

"Fine."

The captain stood up and crossed over to the door. He yanked it open. "O'Neill, get in here!"

He stepped back and a moment later Liam strode in the door, his face scrunched up with concern. He glanced at Mark and if anything he only looked more uncomfortable.

The captain shut the door.

"O'Neill, you know why you're in here?" he barked.

"No, sir," Liam said.

"I wanted to know where you thought you were going just now."

"Out on patrol...to work," Liam said.

"Not dressed like that you're not."

Liam looked over his uniform, clearly trying to figure out what was wrong. Mark bit his lip to keep from smiling.

"I want you to go home and don't come back here until you're dressed properly," the captain said.

"Yes, sir," Liam said, still clearly confused.

The captain reached into a desk drawer and pulled something out. He tossed it to Liam who caught it in midair.

"You'll be needing that."

"A detective's shield?" Liam asked.

"Yeah, that's the good news, you just made detective. Congratulations."

Liam's mouth dropped open in shock. After a moment he managed to ask, "What's the bad news?"

"You'll be partnering with this piece of work here," the captain said, pointing to Mark.

Mark smiled.

Liam stepped forward and for one awkward moment Mark was afraid the other officer was going to hug him. Instead he held out his hand. "It will be my honor."

"Mine, too," Mark said, standing and shaking.

"God save us all," the captain muttered. "Now both of you, get out of here and go catch some bad guys."

Cindy hung up the phone and turned back to her computer. It was strange to be back at work like nothing had happened. She had been kidnapped...again...and they had found priceless artwork and treasures worth hundreds of millions of dollars in the process ending a decades long search for some of those items. She felt like somehow it should be totally life changing.

But yet, here she was back at her desk fielding phone calls about when different events were going to be happening and struggling to figure out the calendar for the next month.

"This is never how it would have ended if it was a movie," she sighed to herself.

The front door opened and she looked up. Dave was standing there, his face a mask of despair and desperation.

"What's wrong?"

"I can't deal with Roy and Gus's arguing anymore," he said. "It's just too much."

"They're fighting again?"

"Yes, right now."

"Where are they?" Cindy asked.

"In the sanctuary."

"They're arguing in the sanctuary?" she asked, feeling something inside of her let loose.

"Yes."

"That's it," Cindy said. "No more." She pushed back from her chair and headed to the door.

"What are you doing?" Dave asked.

"Something that someone should have done a long time ago," Cindy said, setting her jaw.

She walked out the door and headed at a brisk pace for the sanctuary. Once inside she moved a few paces in. She stepped over the place where seemingly a lifetime ago she'd found a dead body lying behind the last pew. That moment replayed itself vividly in her memories.

The pain, the terror, and Jeremiah, a stranger to her then, coming to her rescue.

Roy and Gus were standing at the front, just in front of the pulpit, gesturing wildly.

"You're crazy. It won't fit," Roy was saying.

"It will if you'd just let me move things around a little for the service. It's not like anything is bolted down. Why are you being so stubborn about this?" Gus asked.

"And why do you want to mess up what we already have, just to satisfy your own ego?"

They were so intent on each other that they didn't even notice her as she marched down the aisle. When she drew close to them, she thundered, "Enough! This is the house of God and that might not mean anything to you two, but it does to me."

They both turned and looked at her in surprise. Roy recovered first. "This is a private conversation."

"No, it's not, and that's the problem. You two have been at each other's throats for years and you might like to delude yourself into thinking that it's no one else's business, but it affects all of us. Geanie quit because of your fighting. Dave is about to. Your inability to get along with each other is hurting everyone around you and you're both too selfish and pigheaded to see it. You might not have a problem hurting others and ultimately tearing this church apart, but I have a real problem with it."

"I think you're being overly dramatic," Gus said.

"No!" she shouted. She stepped forward and shoved a finger in his chest. "You are being overly blind and selfish. Both of you are," she said, turning on Roy and thumping him in the chest as well just in case he thought she wasn't talking to him, too. "If you weren't you'd see the pain and the anxiety you've caused, you'd realize how much stress and difficulty you've brought upon us all when you drove Geanie to quit.

"Now, I don't know how this whole thing between the two of you started, but I know it's been going on for years and it's time to stop. You know what today is? It's Yom Kippur. It's the Day of Atonement and that means it's the day to get right with God and to start anew. I'm beginning to think the two of you could learn a little bit from our neighbors."

"We're not Jewish," Roy said.

"No. Which means you have even less excuse. We don't have one day for atonement, for reconciliation with God and a few days to reconcile with others. It's our duty, our responsibility, to God and our fellow man to make every day Yom Kippur. Ephesians 4:26 says 'Let not the sun go down upon your wrath'. And Jesus himself said, 'Judge not, and ye shall not be judged: condemn not, and ye shall not be condemned: forgive, and ye shall be forgiven.' Do either of you remember that?"

"Luke 6:37," Gus muttered, dropping his eyes.

"Oh, so you, at least, remember it. Look, I get it, the two of you don't like each other, you don't see eye-to-eye. Fine, but don't take it out on the rest of us, don't make us suffer because of it. Either you shake hands right now, ask each other's forgiveness, forgive each other and pledge to try to work things out more peaceably in the future or both of you quit now and go work somewhere else where you might not poison everything around you."

She stopped and glared at both of them.

"I never realized I was hurting everyone else, I just didn't think," Gus said, looking ashamed. "I just get my mind set on things and I dig in my heels and never stop to look at who I might be trampling on. I am so sorry," he said, lifting his eyes to look at Cindy. She could read the misery there.

"That's nice, but I'm not the one you need to ask forgiveness from."

"You're right. I'll go apologize personally to Geanie as soon as we're done here." He took a deep breath and turned to Roy. "I am so sorry. I was wrong to fight with you instead of trying to find a peaceful compromise. I don't know where things went wrong between us, but I know that my stubbornness is mostly to blame. I am so very sorry for all the trouble and hurt I've caused. Can you ever forgive me?"

Roy cleared his throat, "I forgive you."

"Thank you," Gus said. "That means a lot to me. I hope we can just start fresh. You're right, I'm trying to change too much about the Christmas pageant too soon in my zeal to do something fresh and new. There are a lot of little things that we could do that would accomplish the same thing without causing so many problems. I'll get to work on that."

"Good," Cindy said, feeling better. She reached out and touched Gus's shoulder and he smiled gratefully at her. She then turned expectantly to Roy.

He just stared at Gus without saying anything. A minute passed in silence.

Finally Cindy asked, "And what do you want to say to Gus?"

"I don't need your forgiveness, nor do I want it."

Cindy couldn't hold back a gasp. She thought the two men were actually getting somewhere. He turned and looked at her. "You are right, though. This place is toxic. I'm leaving."

He turned and exited through the side door.

Gus and she just stared after him.

"I didn't see that coming," Cindy whispered.

"Me either," Gus said.

Cindy turned around and jumped. There, lined up at the back of the sanctuary, was the rest of the staff, standing, watching.

"How long have they been there?" she asked.

"They came in right after you," Gus said. "They heard everything."

Cindy felt slightly dizzy. What had she just done? She had lambasted the head pastor and he had just quit. What would the others say?

She walked slowly up the aisle, her heart in her throat.

Dave lifted his hands and clapped them together. She stared at him, wondering if he'd lost his mind. Then, suddenly, all of them were applauding.

She walked toward them as one in a dream. When she was close Sylvia stepped forward and hugged her. "Thank you," she said softly. "Someone had to do it."

Gus came up next to her. The applause stopped. "I need to ask everyone's forgiveness," he said. "I'm arrogant, proud, opinionated, and stubborn. And I realize those are my good traits."

Dave smiled at that.

"I know it can't have been easy to work with me the last few years. I'm sorry. If you can all forgive me,

I'd love to stay. If you can't, I understand and I'll go, for the good of the church."

Dave stepped forward and embraced him. "I forgive you."

Sylvia hugged him next. "I forgive you."

"We'd like you to stay," Jake, the associate pastor, said as he, too, embraced Gus. Then he turned to Cindy and hugged her as well. "I'm sorry. I should have been the one to put an end to the feuding."

"It's okay," Cindy said, dazed.

Danielle, the children's pastor and the janitor Ralph both stepped forward to embrace Gus as well.

"I just need to call Geanie now," Gus said.

"No need," Geanie spoke up from the doorway.

Cindy looked up at her roommate, startled.

"I was supposed to be meeting with Sylvia," Geanie said.

"I was going to beg her to come back. I hadn't filed any paperwork yet," Sylvia said.

Gus walked over and hugged her. Cindy couldn't hear what they said to each other, but when they broke apart Geanie was wiping a tear from her eye. She cleared her throat. "I guess we're all staying," she said, her voice shaky.

Everyone cheered and Cindy grabbed the back of a pew for support. Her relief that Geanie was coming back was overwhelming. Maybe this was all going to work out after all.

"Okay," Jake said finally. "It's lunchtime. So, I only have one question. Where are we going out to eat, because food's on me."

This was met by more cheers and a quick decision to take two cars and go to the local steakhouse. Everyone scattered to grab purses and wallets and lock everything up before agreeing to meet back up in the parking lot.

Five minutes later Cindy was piling into a car with Geanie, Sylvia, and Dave. Everyone was talking at once and the excitement was palpable. It felt like everyone had a new lease on life. It was utterly amazing.

"You realize this will go down in church legend as the day the secretary fired the pastor?" Dave said, turning around from the front passenger seat to give her a huge grin.

Cindy groaned. "Great, that's just what I needed."

"Maybe not, but it's what everyone else did," he said, turning serious. "Again, thank you. I'm sorry it fell to you to show them that that what they were doing was destructive."

"Me, too," Cindy said with a sigh. "At least that part's over."

"Yeah, now we just have to tell the congregation, notify the higher ups, and see who we get sent as a replacement," Sylvia said.

Cindy groaned. "I can't even think about that at the moment."

"You shouldn't. Today's a victory and you need to celebrate it for what it is," Sylvia said.

"Things are going to be changing around here," Geanie noted.

Cindy reached over and hugged her. "At least you'll still be here."

"Amen," Sylvia and Dave chorused from the front.

"That was a nightmare I was not prepared to deal with," Sylvia admitted. "Do you have any idea how hard you'd be to replace given everything you do?"

"Hmmm...I think I sense a raise coming my way," Geanie said.

"Not likely," Dave laughed. "I haven't seen one in three years."

"Well, maybe if you worked harder," Sylvia said tartly, "instead of goofing off."

"I'm the youth pastor, goofing off is my entire job description," Dave said.

Cindy laughed. The world wasn't ending. In fact in so many ways it felt like it was just beginning. She couldn't remember the words Jeremiah had told her days ago, but she smiled and said, "Happy Jewish New Year! May we all be sealed for a great year."

There was another chorus of "amens" followed by more joking and teasing.

Everything was changing, and she realized that wasn't a bad thing.

She leaned back in her seat and smiled.

Lunch ended up taking most of the rest of the day. By the time they made it back to the office there was just enough time to really close up shop for the night. Cindy drove home, heated herself up a frozen dinner, and settled down to watch some television.

It should have been relaxing, at the very least mind-numbing, but she couldn't find any kind of release from the frustration she was feeling. She finally turned off the television in disgust.

She glanced out the window just in time to see the sun setting. Fall was upon them, sunset was coming earlier it seemed each night.

Sunset. That meant Yom Kippur was over.

She got up and changed clothes. Maybe talking to Jeremiah would help her sort out how she was feeling. She drove to the synagogue, thinking he might not have left yet.

When she pulled into the parking lot and saw his car still there she knew she was right. She got out and leaned against it. A breeze was blowing and the cool air felt good against her skin.

She let her mind wonder, thinking about that breeze and where it was coming from, how many other people it had touched. The world was a big place, but her own little piece of it felt like it was shrinking. It upset her, unnerved her in a way few things ever had.

She heard a footstep and it shook her out of her reverie. Jeremiah was walking toward her.

"Surprise," she said.

"A nice one. What are you doing here?"

"I just realized it was sunset. That means the Days of Awe are officially over, right?"

"Yes, it does. They are."

"Everything go okay?"

He tilted his head and shrugged. "My people got everything they were expecting and I did everything that was required of me in my official capacity."

"How about personally?" she asked.

"Not as spiritual or as productive as I would have liked," he admitted. "Seems I had some pressing things on my mind."

"I'm sorry," she said.

"It's not your fault," he said, reaching out to brush a strand of hair out of her face. "How about you? Are you doing okay?" he asked.

"Not really."

"What's wrong?"

"I don't know, I guess I'm just out of sorts. All these huge, epic things happened and then I wake up today and it's like back to life as normal. It just seems wrong somehow. Like somehow this almost isn't even my life. Do you know what I mean?"

He gave her a strange smile. "More than you could possibly guess."

"So, you're saying I'm not alone?"

He reached out and took her hand, and gave it a squeeze. "That's exactly what I'm saying."

She smiled. "Well, I guess that makes me feel better. I just wish we knew what to do about it."

"We could run off to Paris, leave right now."

"Very funny," she said, with a laugh.

He wasn't laughing, though.

"What, seriously?"

"You know, we get so caught up in our lives, these little circles that we run around in, the cycles of days and weeks and years. Sometimes we forget that we need to shake things up, dream great dreams, dare to take risks. If you want to change your life, then do it."

The very thought took her breath away, and suddenly for the first time in her life, she truly envied her brother Kyle. His entire life was about the adventure, living the big moments, chasing the great dreams, and daring to take the risks others only wished they could.

Then, another thought surprised her. Maybe someday she'd be more like him. Maybe that wouldn't even be a bad thing.

"You know, Kyle's never found treasure," she said.

"And Kyle's never solved murders or tangled with international art thieves," Jeremiah pointed out.

"Or been kidnapped. Twice. Who would have thought it? My life might just be more exciting than his," she said with a grin.

"Excellent!"

"What about you? What secret dreams do you entertain?" she asked.

He hesitated, then gave her a big smile. "What can I say? Everything I want in the world is right here."

Look for

IN THE PATHS OF RIGHTEOUSNESS

Coming Summer 2013

Debbie Viguié is the New York Times Bestselling author of two dozen novels including the *Wicked* series, the *Crusade* series and the *Wolf Springs Chronicles* series co-authored with Nancy Holder. Debbie also writes thrillers including *The Psalm 23 Mysteries,* the *Kiss* trilogy, and the *Witch Hunt* trilogy. When Debbie isn't busy writing she enjoys spending time with her husband, Scott, visiting theme parks. They live in Florida with their cat, Schrödinger.